She'd known the n

And she was pretty su~~~~~~~~~~~~~~~~~~~~, she would have been a more-than-enthusiastic participant.

And that scared her on a deeper level. Because it had been her that had been thinking of kissing him.

Thank God that hadn't happened. Because she didn't see how she'd be able to face him again if he'd reeled back in shock and dismay. Instead, it was her who'd reeled back in dismay at her thoughts a few minutes ago.

Somehow she was able to walk out of the coffee shop on legs that were shaking. Almost as much as her confidence in her ability to maintain a celibate lifestyle. Because the moment he'd stroked her hand, the moment he'd given her that look…celibacy had been the furthest thing from her mind.

Had she been crazy to think he'd felt the same thing?

Dear Reader,

What is your greatest fear? Loss? Financial insecurity? Being alone?

Saraia Jones knows firsthand about loss. She lost her husband to an infection when their twin girls were only three months old. And years later, the man she was dating walked out on her. Since then, she's battled with the fear of loss. Enter Eoin Mulvey, whose good looks and compassion tempt her to try again. But Eoin has a secret that could destroy any chance they have of being together.

Thank you for joining Sari and Eoin as they battle through the fear of loss and learn to make hard choices. This special couple won my heart from the moment they stepped onto the pages of this book. I hope you love reading about their journey as much as I loved writing it.

Love,

Tina Beckett

A DADDY FOR THE MIDWIFE'S TWINS?

———

TINA BECKETT

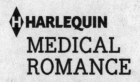

HARLEQUIN
MEDICAL
ROMANCE

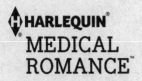

HARLEQUIN®
MEDICAL
ROMANCE™

Recycling programs
for this product may
not exist in your area.

ISBN-13: 978-1-335-59516-4

A Daddy for the Midwife's Twins?

Copyright © 2023 by Tina Beckett

All rights reserved. No part of this book may be used or reproduced in
any manner whatsoever without written permission except in the case of
brief quotations embodied in critical articles and reviews.

This is a work of fiction. Names, characters, places and incidents
are either the product of the author's imagination or are used fictitiously.
Any resemblance to actual persons, living or dead, businesses,
companies, events or locales is entirely coincidental.

For questions and comments about the quality of this book,
please contact us at CustomerService@Harlequin.com.

Harlequin Enterprises ULC
22 Adelaide St. West, 41st Floor
Toronto, Ontario M5H 4E3, Canada
www.Harlequin.com

Printed in U.S.A.

Three-time Golden Heart® Award finalist
Tina Beckett learned to pack her suitcases almost
before she learned to read. Born to a military family,
she has lived in the United States, Puerto Rico,
Portugal and Brazil. In addition to traveling, Tina
loves to cuddle with her pug, Alex; spend time with
her family; and hit the trails on her horse. Learn
more about Tina from her website or friend her on
Facebook.

Books by Tina Beckett

Harlequin Medical Romance

California Nurses
The Nurse's One-Night Baby

Visit the Author Profile page
at Harlequin.com for more titles.

For my family. I love you.

PROLOGUE

EOIN MULVEY HELD the envelope in his hand. He didn't open it…already knew the words inside by heart. It was the twentieth such envelope he'd received. One for every year since his diagnosis when he'd been eighteen years old. And every year he had a choice—continue storage or sign the paperwork to discontinue it altogether.

At thirty-eight, Eoin was pretty sure he wasn't going to suddenly get the urge to have biological children of his own. And since he didn't seem to have the best track record in the relationship department, why should he think he'd be any better at being a father?

He'd mentally given himself until he was forty to decide one way or the other. But that deadline was rapidly approaching. Would two more years really make that much of a difference in his life? More importantly, was it what he wanted?

He'd thought it was when he and his girl-friend, Lucy, had met and gotten together. But then she'd pressured him to make that decision last year, just before their breakup—saying if he wanted children now was the time. But suddenly he hadn't felt ready. And it looked like now that that had been the right choice. Because they'd called it quits less than two months later. Not necessarily over the banked sperm, but it sure hadn't won him any points.

Going over to his stack of mail that was his "take care of later" pile, he tossed the envelope onto the top. He was pretty sure it was just going to end up being shredded and thrown in the trash, but he'd give himself a day or two to decide whether or not to take action. He could donate the sperm, but he wasn't sure he wanted to do that either. He'd always thought that someday he'd be a father, that someday he'd know when the time was right to have kids of his own.

But when Lucy had tried to insist, some-thing had held him back. Maybe it was the thought of being somehow tied to the same woman for the rest of his life. And if he'd agreed to have a baby with her, that was exactly what would have happened. Because he would never abandon his own child.

It was a moot point because they hadn't pursued that path. So for now, he would simply continue to help deliver other peoples' babies and live that joy vicariously through them.

It was enough. It had to be. Because, at the moment, he saw no other viable options.

CHAPTER ONE

"I THINK HE'S HERE!"

The clinic had been quieter than normal this morning, with no actively laboring moms. Just the usual prenatal appointments. But that could change at any time.

Saraia Jones glanced up from the text she'd just gotten from one of her twins' preschool teachers and looked at the receptionist. "Who's here?"

"The new doctor. He's a cute one too." The happily married mother of four grinned. "Better be careful, Sari. This one isn't on the brink of retirement."

Rolling her eyes, she gave her friend a look that she hoped conveyed her disapproval with this line of discussion.

The clinic's last obstetrician had retired last month, and they'd had a devil of a time getting another one to take them on. After all, a free—well, almost free—birthing center didn't bring in a whole lot of revenue other than grants and fundraising efforts, so they couldn't offer the huge salaries that some of the hospitals in the Charleston area could afford.

So when one of the largest teaching hospitals in the city had said they had a doctor who was willing to donate a portion of his time—until the clinic found someone more permanent—she'd been more than thrilled. Especially since she'd heard of the man—whose expertise in difficult deliveries was well known, even to Sari, who partnered with women who wanted to go the midwife/doula route. Almost all of them did, since that was one of Grandview Birthing Center's major draws: as few interventions as possible for a safe delivery. An option she wished she'd had when she'd been giving birth to her own girls.

Before either of them could say anything else, the front door swung open, and Saraia did her best not to do a double take. Heidi was right. The man was…well, a hunk. There was no lab coat in sight, but she was pretty sure that even if he wasn't dressed in snug black jeans and a maroon polo shirt, he would have garnered the same reaction. With wavy brown hair that fell over his forehead and a craggy line emblazoned in one cheek, there was something about him that made her eyes want to visit the various landmarks in his face for far longer than they should.

Forcing herself to maintain eye contact instead, she walked over to him. "Dr. Mulvey?"

"Yes. That's me." He paused, that line in his cheek going into action as he obviously waited for her to identify herself. And although she had earned her Doctor of Nursing practice degree as well as being a certified midwife, she didn't use the title of *Doctor*. She was proud to be a nurse midwife and didn't need anything other than knowing she was well equipped to help her patients.

"I'm Saraia Jones, and this is Heidi Midland. Thanks for being willing to come."

He nodded, acknowledging the other woman. "Nice to meet you both. I'm here to help—so, saying that, I'm ready to jump in with both feet. So which one of you can tell me how to do that?"

Sari had to admire his work ethic, but she needed to set him straight. "That would be me. And I'm glad to hear you're ready to go to work, but I do want to warn you that you probably won't see as much action as you would at your hospital. We hope that yours is more of an advisory role."

"Advisory."

"Most of our laboring patients have educated and prepped themselves from the moment they decided to use midwives. They want a more natural birthing experience," she explained. "We have a system that works for us, and things normally run according to plan. It's when they don't, for whatever reason, that we like to have an ob-gyn on hand to assist. We'd rather not have to transport our patients unless absolutely necessary."

"I see. And how many times have you found it…necessary?"

One of his brows raised in a way that made her stiffen. They did not willfully withhold treatment options from their patients, if that was what he was insinuating. Sari wanted a good outcome on each and every delivery.

"Not often," she said. "We have a surgical suite and an anesthesiologist on the premises, in case there's an emergency. We can even do C-sections, if needed."

"Good to know. And if there's more than one emergency at the same time?"

She blinked and did her best not to let his questioning offend her—because he was right. If two women went into crisis at the same time, it would be difficult to handle. But they screened their expectant moms pretty carefully and did their best to space them out so that they didn't have twenty women all due in the same month. When their docket was full, it was full, and as much as she hated to turn moms away, she did so on a regular basis, referring them to another birthing center in the area.

"So far that hasn't happened. Again, we have a system in place to try to avoid those kinds of scenarios. I'll explain all that to you as we tour the facility."

Out of the corner of her eye she saw Heidi sidestepping back to her post, as if trying to get out of range. Evidently Sari hadn't done as good a job as she'd thought of hiding her slight tickle of irritation. She didn't even know the man and she was already expecting him to try to take over. Maybe because the previous doctor had been so on board with their mission that Sari had a hard time believing that any other obstetrician could be as easygoing. Especially one who she'd heard specialized in surgical delivery techniques. Where his expertise had thrilled her moments earlier, it now made her wary. Would he somehow imagine an emergency lurking around every corner?

From her experience some doctors viewed birthing centers as direct competition to hospitals. And maybe they were. But that wasn't her intention. Sari tended to see it as more of a partnership where they both could help their patients have the best experience possible.

She wasn't trying to put hospital maternity wards out of business. She simply wanted to offer another option. One that she wanted every woman to have available to her. The only "right" delivery was a safe one. One where the mother felt most comfortable and in charge of her body. Her own hospital delivery had been less than optimal. Her baby girls had been delivered in a cold surgical environment that had focused on "safe and sanitary" but had done very little to accommodate her own wishes, which had been a quiet room in which she could labor with her husband. Instead the constant checks and hustle and bustle had made her feel like she had no control over anything, not even whether or not to have the C-section where her twins had been delivered.

She didn't want that for her patients.

And since Dr. Mulvey was here, he must've agreed with that philosophy, right? At least in part. So maybe she should cut him some slack. Especially if she expected him to do the same.

Options were good, right? At least her one and only romantic partner since her husband's death had thought so when he'd come to her one night and said he'd thought they should keep their options open as far as dating other people. Sari had taken that as a euphemism for saying they were at a dead end ahead as far their relationship went, and since she wasn't interested in being a "booty call" when no one else was available, she'd broken things off. When he'd called her a few weeks later, she simply hadn't answered. Or any of the other times he'd tried to contact her.

Her girls had been devastated at losing someone who'd seemed fun to be around. They would be even more devastated if they learned that they had been part of the reason

Max had balked. He hadn't been sure he'd wanted a ready-made family. At least that was the feeling she'd gotten when her babysitter had gotten sick one night and they'd ended up having to take the girls with them to the movies. Max hadn't been happy, although he'd done his best to hide it. But their very next date had ended with the "options open" suggestion. She would never do that to her girls ever again.

"Are you ready?"

Dr. Mulvey's voice pulled her from her thoughts, and she forced a smile. "Of course."

Time to play nice with the doctor. She was proud of their little facility, and as they walked she pointed out the things they'd worked so hard to achieve in the four years they'd been here in Charleston. "We have five labor-and-delivery rooms and four exam rooms."

"Have you ever had five patients laboring at one time?"

"Have you ever been able to convince a baby not to come at a certain time?"

He grinned. "Well, I've tried a time or two, but they're usually pretty insistent."

His smile made something shift inside of

her, and she couldn't stop her own lips from curving. "Same here. But in answer to your question we don't typically have someone in every room, unless they're all at different stages of labor," she said. "And we have four other midwives who work at the clinic— you'll meet Miranda, who is due in at ten. We normally have two midwives on duty at any one time, and one is on call. We do that so that we all have at least one true day off a week."

"And where do I fit in with that roster?"

This was where it got a little tricky. Despite the hectic schedules that came with being a doctor, most didn't do well with just sitting around twiddling their thumbs. "If I say 'hopefully nowhere,' will it bother you? Although you might have a line of patients outside of your little cubicle once they realize you're working here."

He shot her a look, and she realized how that last comment had sounded. She certainly hadn't meant to imply that his looks might have something to do with that—although the thought had sure as heck crossed her mind.

"And just why might they be lining up outside of my cubicle?" he asked.

Heat rushed into her face. He'd caught her meaning. Oh, Lord, this tour was not going like she'd envisioned it. Heidi would've been gleeful if she could see them.

Sari decided to tweak what she'd said. "It was a joke. There aren't a whole lot of men who go into midwifery. But seriously," she said, "you might be called in to do prenatal exam *if* one of us has a questionable presentation. But most of our moms want to see the midwife who will eventually deliver her baby, so we try not to switch it up. The goal is to have the same midwife follow their patient from the beginning until delivery. It's the one reason we'll call someone in on their day off. And all four of us are fine with that."

"All four of you. I see."

Sari realized she'd inadvertently made it sound like an "us versus you" atmosphere. That wasn't what she'd wanted to impart. And the last thing she wanted to do was start this off as an adversarial relationship. She wanted them to be a team working toward the same goal: accommodating the mother's wishes while having a safe and healthy delivery. She was making a mess of this whole thing, and that wasn't like her. Maybe Heidi was right.

Maybe his looks were affecting her—and not in a good way.

She cleared her throat and tried not to look at him. "I promise we will pull you in if we have any questions about a patient's well-being. Our goal is to offer a stress-free environment for both mom and baby. But if safely providing that becomes impossible, we won't hesitate to transfer her care to you."

"I'd rather not be sitting here all day doing nothing, when I could be back at the hospital helping patients," Dr. Mulvey said. "Is there a reason you don't just have an on-call doctor?"

"We've tried that. But sometimes there's a need for immediate intervention. Trying to wait even fifteen minutes to get someone here would put lives in danger. I'm sorry if your hospital didn't make that clearer, and I'll understand if you decide this isn't for you."

She held her breath. It had been so hard to find someone willing to help—she would be upset with herself if she inadvertently chased him off.

"No, that's not it," he said. "And you'll find that once I commit to something I follow it through to the end."

Unlike Max, who'd professed his undying

love for her and her girls and then decided he'd wanted to see what else was out there?

God, this was nothing like that. Why did she keep making those kinds of comparisons? Maybe because Eoin Mulvey seemed less than thrilled with what his relationship with the clinic would be.

Again, that had nothing to do with her, other than work environment. If he truly had a problem with his role with the clinic, he'd have to take that up with his hospital.

But that would leave them without a doctor again. And part of the requirements of the board was that they had a doctor physically at the clinic for a certain number of hours a week and that one would be on call for the remainder of the time. The on-call doctors they had no trouble finding, since they weren't called into the clinic except for on rare occasions. But they'd had trouble finding one who was willing to hang out there for very little pay and very little action. Maybe she should at least try to make it sound like she wanted him.

Her face heated again at how her brain had put together that last sentence.

Dr. Mulvey's head tilted as he studied her. "What?"

"Just thinking." What else could she say? "I'd be happy for you to be in the room for the exams and deliveries for the next couple of weeks, if you'd like. That way you can get a better feel for what the clinic does and how we screen patients."

He seemed to mull that over for a few seconds before responding. "That would work. And what would I do during the deliveries?"

"Honestly?" She waited.

"Preferably." Again that line in his face deepened as his lips twitched.

"The fewer medical interventions we have, the better. At least as far as the clinic's mission statement goes. But maybe you can observe some of our different options—at least if the patient doesn't object to your presence. Maybe you'll find some tools you can add to your tool belt."

"Maybe."

He didn't sound convinced, and she couldn't blame him. His training dealt with difficult scenarios, and she was pretty sure he was always thinking three steps ahead in every delivery he participated in. It was probably etched in his DNA by now.

"If you disagree with a decision, maybe hold that thought—unless it's a life-or-death situation—until you're able to talk to one of us in private about it," she said. "I'd rather our patients not feel we're at odds with each other, even though we might be at times." This time she allowed a smile of her own to seep through.

"What? I can't even imagine that happening." The heavy irony infusing those words made her laugh. Then he added, "But I think I can live with your suggestion."

Those words made her relax. She couldn't ask for more than that. "Great, then let's take that tour I promised you."

"Since I'm yours for the day, that sounds like a plan."

She swallowed. He wasn't hers. He was the clinic's. And no matter how devastatingly attractive he might be, Sari needed to remember that. Especially since Evie had evidently started crying this morning and told her teacher that she missed Max. Her teacher had sent her a concerned text. And now Sari had to write back and explain the situation. A situation that should have been over and done six months ago, when they'd broken up. But evidently for at least one of her daughters it wasn't that simple.

Of course it wasn't. But she wouldn't make the same mistake twice. And that mistake was introducing Evie and Hannah to someone who could hurt them. Again.

Eoin was actually impressed with the facility, although he'd had his doubts when he'd originally agreed to volunteer. But he'd always been curious as to how birthing centers like these operated, and he prided himself on being open-minded and non-judgmental. Although his preconceived notions were coming through. He'd heard them a couple of times when he'd commented on this or that or asked a question. Each time it had happened, he'd cringed, realizing he wasn't as impartial as he'd claimed he was. Surprisingly, although Saraia Jones had thrown him a peeved-looking glance when they'd first started out, she hadn't snapped at him, even when he might have deserved it. In fact, she'd seemed to relax, her dark hair sliding across her face when she'd glanced up at him a time or two, making something tighten in him.

But he forced himself to concentrate on what she'd said about the clinic. And it was impressive. The place was immaculate, although the plants propped on shelves or lining the hallways made him tilt his head. His hospital did the fancy bedding and so forth quite well, but even he could admit it didn't look as cozy or inviting as the birthing rooms at Grandview. All of their medical equipment was tucked out of sight, like the lights that were rolled behind screens or the other paraphernalia that was closed inside of a big antique-looking hutch.

If someone walked into one of these rooms, they would swear that it was an ordinary bedroom, not a room where extraordinary things happened. Maybe Saraia was right. Maybe there was a tool or two that he was missing in his own practice. But he was geared to dealing with births where time was of the essence, and having to stop and pull something out of its hiding place? He wasn't quite sold on that. At least not yet.

"You said you have water births as well?" Eoin asked.

"Yep, it's just in this last room."

Saraia unlocked a door on their right and waited for him to go ahead of her. He did and then stopped. This room looked like some kind of cabana. The tile on the floor had the appearance of wood planking, which extended halfway up the walls, giving it a warm and inviting look and yet was undoubtedly easy to sterilize. There were soft curtain-like fabrics draped around the space and an acrylic birthing pool placed in the middle of the room. Again, it didn't look like any delivery room he'd ever seen.

As if expecting the question, Saraia spoke up. "The soft-scaping—such as the draperies—are taken down and replaced with sanitized ones after the completion of each birth. And the moms can wear their own clothing—or not. Whatever makes them the most comfortable."

"And the benches around the tub are for…?"

"They're a place where family members can sit and observe or participate in the birth experience, which many families choose to do."

Eoin's brows went up. "How often is this room used?"

"It depends on the month. It's not quite as popular as some of the other rooms, but we felt it important to offer it as an option."

Which didn't answer his question. As if she realized that, she went on to say, "We probably use this room twice a week at the moment. Sometimes more."

"And changing out those 'softscapes,' as you put it. Who does that?"

Saraia glanced around the room. "Our cleaning crew. The same ones who change the bed linens and towels. They're sent out to a laundry service."

"So if this room starts being used daily, you have enough staff to keep up with the demand?" The words came out sounding like a challenge, and he hadn't meant them to.

She frowned. "We try to keep our numbers pretty steady, although we do have more patients some months than others. For their own safety, we have a cap on how many we babies we can deliver at any given time. I'll admit it's a juggling act, but hospitals sometimes find themselves scrambling too when an unexpected number of patients go into labor at the same time."

"Yes, I agree. That probably wasn't a fair question."

Saraia's face tilted, and there went that hair slide again. It looked soft and touchable, and his fingers tingled. Eoin forced them to curl at his sides.

"No, it was fair. And I want to present a realistic picture to anyone who walks through those doors. It's one reason we don't have a blowup-style birthing pool. It's easier to clean the room and the pool when it's hard acrylic."

He'd figured that might be the case, although most of the ones he'd seen were a taller version of an inflatable kiddie pool. Unlike the beds that could be stripped and remade, a pool seemed like a more complicated process to sanitize. But this didn't look that way. Solid white, it was cloverleaf in shape, each leaflet having what looked like a separate function with different configurations that would support a laboring mom in various positions.

But there was a picture hanging on the wall of how the room might look when it was in use. Eoin walked over to it, seeing a smiling family gathered around water that looked a little bluer than it might in real life. His mouth twisted in amusement. "I take it you don't tint the water with food coloring."

She sighed. "No. That was probably artistic license—although I never really noticed that before. It was actually the photo used by the pool manufacturer. We just liked the design so much that we tried to recreate the scene. In real life, things don't stay as pretty as they do in pictures."

That was the truth. Eoin had just discarded some pictures of him with Lucy. In all of them, they'd been smiling, either holding hands or with his arm draped around her shoulders. They'd been true enough representations of them at the time, but like Saraia had said, things didn't stay that way.

"No, they don't."

Maybe it was the way he'd said it, but he noticed she gave him a look that seemed to pierce right through the wall he'd erected around himself over the last several months.

Not what he wanted, so he quickly changed the subject. "So do you use a hose to fill the pool?"

Thankfully the tactic worked, and Saraia

went into a detailed explanation of how they'd had to retrofit the room with plumbing last year in order to be able to have a permanent pool. "And just around here is an exam table. That way we don't have to move patients from room to room." She pulled back part of the draperies to reveal another bed like the ones in other rooms.

Eoin was surprised. He'd thought those draperies were simply along the walls of the room. "That is pretty ingenious." He couldn't stop the words from coming out, even though he wasn't fully sold on things he had minimal experience with. He'd have to see it in action before he could pronounce judgment on it one way or the other.

"We thought so," she replied. "Like I said, we copied what they had in the showroom. We really want to keep distractions to a minimum for our patients. We want them to focus on the experience at hand. Part of that is providing a calm, soothing atmosphere where they can do that. But the bed is here in case we need to intervene in some way or when they first come in. I hope my girls can one day have all these options if they ever become moms."

She had children. He hadn't seen a ring on her hand, although that didn't mean anything. She could have a partner. Or maybe she'd chosen to have kids in her own way, such as IVF treatments or something.

"How old are they? Your kids, I mean." Eoin wasn't sure why he'd asked the question, but he couldn't retract it now.

And the smile she gave him was nothing short of dazzling, her white teeth coming down on her lip in a way that cut right through him.

"They're five. Identical twins, actually."

Identical. Probably not IVF, then. Twins were common enough in fertility treatments, but they were normally fraternal twins. "They must keep you busy."

"They do. But in a good way." Saraia glanced around the room. "And it's one of the reasons I'm so passionate about the birthing center. It has all of the things I wish I'd been able to have when I was in labor."

This time he did frown. Pregnancies with twins brought a whole host of possible complications. "You deliver twins here?"

"Some. We screen them carefully. And it's one of the reasons we want an ob-gyn on the premises," she explained. "When I learned I was pregnant, I was scheduled for a C-section...was told it was the safest option. I didn't research that claim. I was already a nurse with a master's degree at a huge hospital at the time, and I trusted my doctor implicitly. But afterward, I heard little murmurs about his Cesarean rate. Evidently it was higher than the average doctor's. It made me sit up and take notice, and then my hus— Well, my life situation changed, and I decided to go back to school and become a midwife."

She touched Eoin's arm, her fingers soft and warm. "I truly believe in this place, and that is not just a line coming from someone who works here."

Her voice rang with a sincerity that seemed to come from deep inside of her. The hand on his arm dropped away, and he found he missed it. So much so that he needed to turn his mind back to why he was here at the clinic. "I believe you," he said. "I hope you'll give me the chance to come to my own conclusions."

"Of course. I wouldn't have it any other way."

Eoin couldn't ask for more than that. And

he hoped she was right about how smoothly things went here. Because all he could think was how it would only take one emergency situation—one death, of mother or baby—to turn this place on its head and undo whatever inroads they'd made with the community.

And when or if that happened, it wouldn't be him who'd be on the street corner proclaiming the benefits of natural childbirth, even though he knew in his heart of hearts that women had been giving birth for a lot longer than the term *ob-gyn* had been around. And it probably wasn't going to come to a screeching halt just because he had some concerns about safety.

So all he could do was sit back and listen—and try to keep everything wrapped up in a nice pretty bow that had nothing to do with his questionable responses to Saraia as a person. It was what he'd come to the birthing center to do. And he would do his damnedest to keep his focus on that.

As long as Saraia and her partners kept safe deliveries as the bedrock of their clinic. If he ever saw something that jeopardized that…

all bets were off. He'd be the first one out the door, and he'd ask his hospital to never partner with them again.

CHAPTER TWO

IT WAS SARAIA'S day off, but one of her patients had unexpectedly gone into labor in the middle of the night. Things had been stable until this morning, but her phone rang at 6:00 a.m. when it became evident that this baby was coming today, whether anyone liked it or not. Since it was Saturday, Evie and Hannah's preschool was closed, and her mom hadn't been available, so she'd packed the girls up and brought them into the center.

It was times like this that she missed David's calm demeanor. He would have sent her on her way and spent the day playing with their daughters. But he wasn't. And sometimes the weight of raising them alone threatened to crush her.

But it was what it was, and Saraia was going to do right by them. Not just for David—from the moment she'd found out she was pregnant she'd committed to doing whatever it took to make sure their needs were met. She just hadn't expected to be doing that alone.

But she was.

Pulling her mind back to the exhausted mother whose pushing phase was going longer than she'd anticipated, Saraia said, "Janie, I'm going to need you to pull your knees to your belly to see if we can give your baby a little more room."

Her patient groaned but did as asked.

"Good. Now, when the next contraction comes, give me a big push."

Within a minute, the baby's head appeared. "Okay, baby's making an appearance, so…"

Before she could get the next words out, the head suddenly disappeared back into the canal. Saraia tensed.

Janie must have sensed something. "What's wrong?"

"Baby's just being a little stubborn." But she knew it could be more than that. The turtle sign, where the head emerged during a contraction but retracted afterward, could be a symptom of shoulder dystocia, where one of the baby's shoulders was trapped behind the pubic bone.

The next contraction came, and the head reappeared but didn't stay there. "Janie, this is very important—I'm going to need you to breathe through the next contraction. Don't push."

She hurriedly pressed the button on the side table that would call for assistance. Heidi, who'd also come in on her day off would know what to do.

Sure enough, her voice came through the intercom. "What can I help with?"

"I need someone in here to assist, and see if you can get Dr. Mulvaney on the line. I'm pretty sure we have a baby whose shoulder is just a bit wedged." She phrased it in a way that hopefully wouldn't alarm the mom but would get across that this was an emergency.

Heidi's voice lowered. "Actually, he's here. He's doing puzzles in the staff lounge with your girls."

Saraia blinked before pushing past the tickle of worry that he was interacting with her daughters and went straight to relief that he was in the building. "Can you ask him to come in here?"

"On it."

She turned her attention back to Janie. "I'm

going to have our doctor come in and check on us, okay? If he gives us the all clear, we'll keep on going as we have been. But we may need to reposition you again and to give that baby a little help."

"A cesarean?" Janie got the words out just before the next contraction hit.

Sari helped her breathe through it before she answered. "I'm not going to lie and say it's not a possibility. But I promise we'll see if we can coax your little one to cooperate before we jump to that option, okay?"

Just as she was finishing the explanation, Eoin appeared in the doorway, faded jeans and a T-shirt that emphasized his broad shoulders and toned arms making her pause for a minute. He wasted no time with chitchat. "What have you got?"

"Possible shoulder dystocia."

Damn. This was not the first delivery she wanted the man to see. She'd wanted a smooth, problem-free, homey atmosphere that would sell him on their clinic's mission statement.

But when had things ever been that easy? And right now was not the time to worry about it, since Eoin had immediately gone to scrub up in the sink.

"Is your surgical suite kept at the ready?" he asked.

"Of course." She glanced at Janie just as the woman's hand gripped hers hard while she did her best not to push as the next contraction hit. The woman was too wrapped up in what was happening with her body to notice what the obstetrician had said.

Eoin dried his hands and snapped on a pair of gloves. "Tell me."

She knew exactly what he meant, and she ran through what was happening: prolonged pushing followed by the turtle sign. "Pregnancy and the early stages of labor went like clockwork."

He nodded. "Shoulder dystocia is one of those that sneaks up on you. The baby isn't oversized?"

"No. We wouldn't have delivered her if that were the case. She weighed just over seven pounds at the last exam. And she's just a few days shy of her delivery date."

"What's her name?"

"Janie."

He came up by her head. "Janie, I'm going

to examine you, and then we're probably going to have to reposition you. It's not going to be comfortable, but I'll do my best to be careful. We all want a healthy baby. Do you know what the sex is yet?"

"N-no…we wanted it to be a surprise. My husband is deployed overseas and couldn't be…" Janie dissolved into tears.

It wasn't Eoin. His words had been surprisingly even and gentle. None of the barking orders that she'd seen from a few of the doctors she'd dealt with when doing her rotations. Not all of them, certainly—most of them were great. But she'd actually heard a doctor ask a patient if she was going to pull him away from his son's soccer game to do the delivery. He'd said it in a joking manner but had griped to the nurses about it outside of the room, asking them to only call him back if absolutely needed.

Saraia got it. Being a doctor was hard. Really hard. So was being a midwife. After all, she'd had to bring her kids to the clinic with her for this delivery, but she wouldn't dream of saying that to Janie. When she'd gone into this profession she'd known what was involved. And she'd talked with Evie and

Hannah a lot about her job. And she loved it. All of it. Whenever it interfered with plans she'd made with her girls, she would seek permission from the newborn's parents to get a picture of the baby and show it to the girls. They always oohed and aahed over the baby.

She kept hold of Janie's hand as Eoin performed his exam. "If we can get the baby rotated just a bit more, we might be able to free up the shoulder."

"I thought the same," Saraia said. "And I will say the baby's presentation was normal last time I examined her. She wasn't sunny-side up, or I would have worked to change things up then."

She sounded defensive, and she hadn't meant it to. Saraia just did not want the obstetrician thinking that she would willingly overlook a glaring red flag. Not that the baby was sunny-side up at this point either. So she wasn't sure why she was even saying anything.

"I didn't imply that you wouldn't." He turned back to the patient. "We're going to help you get up onto all fours."

"I don't think I can."

"We're all going to work together, okay?

Keep your knees bent, and we'll just roll you onto them."

He made it sound so easy. And there still wasn't an ounce of panic in his voice. He'd probably seen so much worse than this. But any time a presentation wasn't absolutely normal, Saraia's heart started pounding—much like it was now. But when that happened, her training tended to kick in and she just pushed through it, doing whatever she had to to make sure the outcome was as good as she could possibly make it. But it sure felt good having him here. A little too good.

Eoin chose that moment to glance at her, his eyes narrowing for a second. "I'll get on the other side of the bed," he said. "See if you can roll her up toward me."

"Got it. Let's do it before the next contraction starts."

Sari pushed with all her might, even as Janie's agonized groans tore at her heart. It would be even worse if Eoin had to go in vaginally to try to turn the baby to dislodge its shoulder.

Once Janie was on her hands and knees, Eoin found the controls that would lower the bed without Sari's help and used his hands to apply firm pressure onto their patient's belly. He stopped when the next contraction came as Sari coached her through it. The all-fours position could open the pelvis more and would hopefully help tip that shoulder off the pelvic bone. They rocked her a couple of times.

"Janie, I'm going to raise the head of the bed," he said. "Keep your knees apart and grip the top of the mattress, okay? And as soon as the next contraction comes, I want you to go ahead and push nice and steady. We're going to see if that baby has worked his or herself loose."

He was putting her into more of a squatting position. It was exactly what Sari would have done, but having a second set of hands was a godsend, especially if the technique didn't work and they had to go to some of the more aggressive maneuvers.

Once their patient was in place, Eoin glanced up at Sari. "Go ahead and get behind her. If the baby progresses, we'll just go with it. If not, we'll need to apply pressure over the pubic bone."

Which would require another repositioning and would hurt like hell. She sent up a quick prayer that what they'd already done would work.

"It's coming," Janie said. This time there was more than a hint of fear in her voice.

The obstetrician nodded to her, and Sari didn't hesitate taking back the lead.

"It's okay, Janie—we're right here. I want you to push slow and easy. Nothing too hard until we make sure the baby is ready to come."

The mom didn't reply but pushed, as Sari leaned an elbow on the mattress behind her and felt for the head. There it was. "Just a little more."

Another push had the head all the way out. Her patient breathed out a loud gasping breath, and Sari's heart was in her throat as she waited to make sure the head would stay out this time.

"It worked." She glanced at Eoin in time to see him nod and step away from the bed.

What? Was he leaving? No. He was just fully handing the reins back to her, and she was grateful. Not only for herself, but for her patient.

"Breathe slow and steady until the next contraction, Janie. We're almost there."

"Are you sure?" The exhaustion was evident in her voice, in the shaking of her limbs as she held herself where she was. A second later, the next contraction was on her and she couldn't say anything else.

"Push." Sari started to slowly count to ten even as she helped ease one shoulder out and then the next. "One more big push. As hard as you can."

Janie did as requested, and things happened really fast now that the shoulders were both delivered. The baby slipped out and into Sari's waiting hands. "And we have a baby."

The new mom sagged, her upper body leaning against the mattress in relief. Which was fine, but Sari didn't want her sitting completely on her knees. Not just yet. "Go ahead and rest, but don't sit."

"Is the baby okay?"

Sari smiled even as the baby squirmed for a second before letting out a loud yowling sound as she took her first breath. "I would say so. You have a little girl, Janie."

"Jacob wanted a girl, wanted to name her Martha after my own mom." Emotions seemed to overwhelm her, and Janie gave a sobbing breath, even as Sari waited for the cord to stop pulsing. Once it did, she clamped it in two spots and then cut it.

"Martha is a beautiful name. You mom would have loved her so much."

Sari learned so much about a patient during the course of a delivery. Like the fact that Janie's mom had died of cancer five years ago at the age of forty-five and that she was missed terribly. But her dad was still living and looking forward to being a grandpa.

"Eoin, can you put the bed back to its normal position so we can help her lie down?"

Sari could do it on her own, but since the obstetrician was in the room, she was going to take advantage of his presence. They put the head of the mattress back down and helped Janie lie on her back. Only then did she put the baby against her mom so they could have some skin-to-skin bonding time. She could clean her up after the afterbirth was delivered.

Which happened in a few minutes. Sari was so busy with what she was doing that when she looked up again, Eoin was gone—it was as if he'd never been here. But she'd never been so glad for someone's presence as she'd been a few moments earlier.

Why was he here anyway? He was only

scheduled for two days a week, and Saturday was definitely not one of them. She hoped he was still in the building so she could thank him and have kind of a debriefing session to unpack what had just happened. All she could hope was that he'd approved of her actions and could see that she wasn't going to overlook symptoms if there was even a hint of a problem. The reality was deliveries could either go without a hitch or things could get dicey very, very quickly. She believed wholeheartedly in what she did. But she believed even more in having a live baby and mom at the end of the day.

With the afterbirth delivered and the baby cleaned up, Sari asked Janie what her plans were for the night. They did have the capability of monitoring mom and baby overnight if the new mom simply needed some rest and peace and quiet. Or if things looked good, she could opt to go home as soon as she was ready. Most of the time, insurance allowed for overnight stays.

"I have a friend who's going to come pick us up as soon as she gets off work." Janie shrugged. "She offered to be my birth coach, but the idea of having someone other than my mom or Jacob next to me… Well, I just couldn't do it."

"I understand. And it's fine—you needed to do what you felt the most comfortable with."

"Thank you." She propped the baby into the crook of her arm and grabbed Sari's hand. "I was so afraid I was going to have to have a cesarean once the doctor came into the room."

"I didn't want that for you," Sari said. "But if he thought it was necessary, I would have deferred to his expertise. But only because I wanted Martha to make it into this world in one piece."

"Me too." Janie glanced around the room. "Did he leave?"

"I think he wanted your delivery to finish the way it started—with just us in the room." At least she hoped that was it. It was one of the reasons she wanted to chat with him.

"Well, please thank him for me if I don't see him again."

"I will." Sari smiled. "Do you want something? A drink? Something to eat?"

"Some yogurt sounds good, if you have some."

"We actually do." The clinic kept a small supply of snacks and drinks on hand to give their new mothers a way to replenish calories lost during delivery. "I'll be back with it in a few minutes, if you're okay."

Janie glanced at her baby, who had already latched onto her mom's breast. "I'm more than okay. I can never thank you enough. Can I have my purse so I can try to video chat with Jacob to give him the news?"

"Absolutely." Sari handed her her purse and waited as she fished her phone out of it. "I'll give you some time alone. Just press the button on the side table if you need me for something. And I'll knock before I come back into the room."

"Thanks again for everything."

"You're more than welcome. I hope you can reach him."

"Yeah. Me too."

With that Sari left the room and went to the front desk, where Heidi was still waiting. "I thought you would have gone home by now."

"No way," Heidi said. "Not without hearing that everything ended up being okay. Eoin says it did."

"And he actually was a great help. Is he still around?"

She nodded at the door to the staff lounge. "I think you-know-who have conned him into coloring with them now."

Saraia stiffened. "He's in with the girls? Again?"

She wasn't sure why it mattered, since he'd already done puzzles with them earlier. But for some reason a little twinge of alarm went through her. Or was that alarm at her own reactions to the man?

"Yep. Evie saw him walk by and stuck her head out to call him over." Heidi grinned. "I don't think it took too much convincing. It's pretty damned adorable of him, if you ask me."

Ugh! Sari didn't want the man to be adorable or in any way attractive to her daughters. She gave an internal laugh because she'd already been affected by him.

But she had seen what could happen when she let a man into their lives. Except she hadn't let this one in, and there wasn't much of a chance that he would be involved in their lives in any meaningful way, other than just some stranger who popped in to do a puzzle with them or color a page from a coloring book.

"Well, I'll happily relieve him of his duties."

"What? Did it not go well in there with Janie?"

She realized Heidi thought she'd meant they weren't going to keep him on at the clinic. And maybe it would have been better if he'd been a pompous, arrogant bastard who snatched at control wherever he went. Well, he had taken charge in there. But only because she'd been glad to let him. And he'd let go of it as soon as he'd seen the crisis was over. She couldn't fault him there. It was what Dr. Eric had done during his time at the clinic, but she hadn't expected Dr. Mulvey to have handed things back over to her so quickly—and without even waiting for the patient to thank him.

A shard of respect worked its way under her skin, and it bothered her for some reason. Maybe because she'd been defensive and on guard when she'd first met him. Did she have a problem with trusting doctors because of what had happened to her during her own birth? She hadn't thought so, but maybe it was something that was swirling around in there without her even being aware of it. It had even taken Dr. Eric some time to gain her confidence, and after he had, she'd been convinced he was an outlier as far as obstetricians went, even though in her head she knew that was probably not the case. There were plenty of obstetricians who worked with hospital midwives on a regular basis. But she'd convinced herself that only happened when it was still in a hospital setting.

A birthing center that was not on hospital property was a different animal. At least that was what she'd told herself.

But right now, she had to go in and rescue Eoin from her daughters before they had his thick wavy hair caught up in multiple rubber bands. She bit her lip at that image.

David would have loved that. But he wasn't here. And Eoin definitely wasn't vying for a position as a significant other for Sari or her girls. Nor did she want him to. She straightened her back and headed to the door of the lounge, taking a deep breath before pushing it open.

No rubber bands in sight. But what was in sight was a tall lanky man hunched over a child-sized table in the corner with a red crayon in his hand.

Her breath left her for a moment as she let herself stare at the sight. And from what she could see, he was coloring a picture of a heart. Sari swallowed, allowing herself to take in the sight for a few seconds more. Max had never deigned to color with her daughters, always telling them he was no good at it and that he wanted them to show them their masterpieces after they were done. But looking back, she was pretty sure he'd just been feeding them a line to get out of interacting with them, although he'd made a show out of telling them how good their pictures looked.

Sari's heart ached over memories that she was now able to see for what they'd been: pretense. Wanting to replace what she'd had with David?

When Hannah and Evie had given Max some pictures to take home, she'd thought it was sweet that he'd folded them up and put them into his pocket. But she'd never seen them displayed in his apartment. Looking back there were so many signs that she'd just ignored because she'd been attracted to the man. She'd only seen what she'd wanted to see.

But not again. Maybe Evie or Hannah had just hounded Eoin into coloring with them. But even if they hadn't, she wasn't going to take any chances. Not this time. Especially with how seeing him there was turning her insides to goo.

She cleared her throat and watched as all their heads jerked around to look at her. She suddenly lost her train of thought as that line in Eoin's face deepened and a tinge of color appeared in his cheeks. Embarrassed to have been caught clutching a crayon? Or sitting at a kiddie table?

Somehow it made the act even more endearing.

Oh, hell. She did not need this. Banishing the softness that was crouched in a corner waiting to infect her heart, Sari nodded at him. "Can I talk to you for a minute?"

A slight furrowing of his brows said it wasn't what he'd expected her to say. But he simply replied, "Sure," before looking at her girls. "I'll have to take a rain check on drawing a unicorn."

"What's a rain check?" asked Hannah.

"It means no."

Evie's response made Sari want to cry. How many times had Max used that term? And Evie was right—it had basically meant he hadn't wanted to do whatever it was they'd been asking him to do.

Eoin slashed a look at her before turning back to Evie. "It actually means it's something I want to do but can't right now. But that I'll do it later."

Hannah tilted her head at him, her smile beaming. "So you'll draw me a unicorn later?"

"I will. The next time I see you with crayons. I promise."

Oh, no. He was *not* going to promise them anything. She wouldn't let him. "Girls, you need to let Dr. Mulvey go. I need to talk to him, and I'm sure he has something to do after that."

He stared at her for a minute before finally nodding. "It would seem that I do." He glanced back at the twins. "Thanks for letting me color with you."

Uncurling his long form from the chair, he paused when Evie jumped to her feet and handed him the paper. "Don't forget to take your heart with you."

He took the colored sheet and smiled. But when he turned away and raised a brow at Sari, it made her feel like he wasn't the one who'd forgotten his heart. She had. Had she turned that hard?

Maybe. But it was for her daughters' own good. After all, she didn't want to end up explaining her relationship status to Evie's and Hannah's teachers every time there was a breakup. Because she didn't expect there to be another one anytime soon. At least not until her girls were at a point when they could understand things a little bit better. Maybe not even then.

She moved into the hallway with him and motioned him out of earshot of Heidi—not that she was one to purposely listen in on conversations. But Sari also didn't want her getting any ideas about Eoin being good dating material or anything.

"Everything okay with Janie and the baby?" he asked.

"Yes, everything went wonderfully. I just wanted to thank you for helping."

"You're welcome. But that's not what this little talk is about, is it?"

Sari bit her lip. How did she ask him not to

color with her daughters without making it sound like she thought he was some kind of pervert? So she decided to evade the subject.

"It is, actually," she said. "I really did appreciate the way you did what you did. You didn't immediately insist on surgery."

He eyed her for a second. "Let's get one thing straight. If I'd come into that room and felt she needed a cesarean, I wouldn't have hesitated to say so."

Lord, how did she always make such a mess of every conversation she had with this man? "I know. But the fact that you were willing to wait and size things up is huge for our patients and means a lot. For me, personally. And with your specialty being at-risk pregnancies, it would be easy to jump right on that bandwagon."

Eoin motioned to one of the benches that flanked the hallway. Once she was seated he sat beside her, hands between his knees, the picture he'd drawn still clutched in one of them. "And maybe my specialty lets me discern between a true medical emergency and a situation where we have a little more time before deciding that surgery is the only way."

She hadn't really thought of it that way.

And she could admit when she was wrong. At least about that.

"I will admit that once you mentioned our surgical suite, I thought you would want to head right in that direction," she said. "I'm glad I was wrong."

"Maybe we can agree to give each other the benefit of the doubt," he said, "since I expected you to fight my suggestions at every turn and was honestly surprised when you didn't."

That made her smile. "Believe me, if I thought you were wrong, you would have heard about it in no uncertain terms."

"I do. Believe you."

They looked at each other, and Sari felt an awareness come into the space that made her swallow. God, she did not want to be attracted to this man. At all. But it was hard when he was just so…unexpected. At every turn. Well, she'd better jump right back onto her high horse and gallop away before things got out of hand.

She nodded at his picture. "Anyway, thanks for entertaining them. But I don't expect you to. They only came today because I couldn't make any other arrangements."

"I know you don't expect me to. But it wasn't like they were asking me to buy them a car. It was just coloring."

Just coloring. Didn't he realize how big that was? And how rarely Evie and Hannah had ever had an adult male sit down and pick up a crayon and interact with them? Or a toy. It was huge. And Evie's response to Hannah's question about a rain check was telling. Her daughter didn't expect anything out of a man. Not anymore.

And neither did Sari. And that made her want to weep. Right now, she just didn't have it in her to tell Eoin to not talk to her girls or to play with them. She couldn't find a way to say it nicely without having to explain why she thought it was such a bad idea for them to get to know him.

Or maybe it was that she couldn't find a way to tell herself that exact thing: That getting to know him—*really* know him—would be a very bad idea. For both her and the girls.

So she settled for a quick informational speech about how Janie and her daughter were progressing and thanked him again for his help. It sounded stilted even to her own ears, but it was all she had. For now.

Or at least until she needed to give him a real warning. And if she did, nothing or no one would stop her from saying what she had to say.

CHAPTER THREE

EOIN SPENT THE next two days doing his regular shift at the hospital. But he had to admit, he kind of missed the calm, laidback atmosphere of Grandview. His days could be rushed and frenetic, with very little time to get to know his patients since they were normally already in crisis by the time he was called in.

When was the last time he'd been able to sit and do puzzles with a child? The last time he'd been able to work side by side with a midwife who was so fiercely protective of her patients? Actually, he rarely worked with midwives at all, but not because he was necessarily against it. But it was just because he was normally rushing someone into the operating room in an attempt to save two lives. And sometimes that wasn't even possible. Every once in a while, it was a matter of deciding who could be saved—mother or baby. Whether it was a car accident where the mom was critically injured or a case where the fetus was in such dire distress that the odds of saving it were astronomical, he could not ever remember being able to turn the situation back over to the referring physician. Or midwife, in this case.

And she'd seemed just as surprised by that as he'd been. Walking out of that room without knowing the outcome had gone against every grain of his being, but somehow he'd sensed it was the right thing—as hard as it had been to do it.

It was as if Saraia had expected him to yank her patient away from her without a second glance. He'd never had to yank anyone. They were normally handed over gladly by a medical professional who would rather not have control over an outcome that sometimes promised only heartache.

And although he'd been busy yesterday and today, it had somehow been harder to face the same cases that he'd once considered a challenge. Seeing the relief on Saraia's face when that baby had slid into her waiting hands, seeing the tearful emotion on Janie's face when she'd realized all was well had done a number on him. He was so used to hardening his heart in order to get the job done that he'd had a hard time allowing it to be softened again when there was a need for it.

And when one of Sari's daughters had asked him to draw a heart, it had been as if the universe had been sending him a reminder that it was okay to sometimes wear his heart on his sleeve. That there were times when it was even good and appropriate to let his feelings show.

It was why that picture was now hanging on his refrigerator, although putting his own crude artwork on display seemed kind of strange. But it was as if he was sending a nod back at some deity, that he would try harder to do just that.

But today had not been the day. He'd just lost a baby whose mom had had an undiagnosed autoimmune disorder.

He sat at the desk in his office, steepled hands supporting his head, and told himself not to try to make sense of it. At seven months' gestation, the baby had been capable of surviving outside of the womb with help. And he'd tried to give that help. The baby girl had been tiny and perfect. So perfect, he'd continued attempts to revive her for several minutes after someone had suggested calling it. Saying those words had been much harder than it might have been just two days ago. Before he'd assisted that mom at Grandview.

Afterward, he'd carried the baby's tiny form to the room where her mother had lain sobbing into her pillow. It had hurt to hand her over, had hurt to witness how carefully she'd cradled her deceased child. To tell her that she could carry another child to term once her condition was under control had been out of the question. At least right then, when the pain of loss had been so real. So raw. So he'd left her there and come back to his office, where he'd dissected his every move during the C-section over and over again. But no matter what scenario he played, he didn't see it ending any differently.

But that didn't help.

Right now, he really wanted to run over to the birthing center and watch a baby being born without a care in the world. Where things ran—mostly—according to plan. Even if he hadn't assisted in the shoulder dystocia, he was reasonably certain that Saraia would have been able to dislodge the baby on her own. But neither of them had known that for a fact. And having a second person nearby had been the right call. One she hadn't hesitated to make, which had surprised him, although he was starting to learn it shouldn't have. Everything he'd heard about Saraia Jones said that she put her patients first. Always.

And yet there were those who said standalone birthing centers put lives at risk. Maybe it was part of the reason he'd volunteered to donate his time—so that he could make up his own mind, rather than go by the thoughts and opinions of others. And it was still too early in the game to call it one way or the other.

He'd seen nothing he disapproved of. Yet. Whether it would still be that way in one month's time or one year's time was yet to be decided.

And Saraia's two daughters had been adorable. Although when one twin had asked the other what *rain check* meant and she'd said, "It means no," it had made him tense. Hopefully their mother hadn't given them that idea. He'd wanted to ask why either child would think that but had known he'd be out of line.

After all, he didn't have children, so why would he think he could tell her how to parent her kids?

He glanced at his calendar. He had nothing else pressing, and he was past his scheduled time. Maybe that was why he was so tired and mentally spent. He'd been here for over nine hours. It was time to go home.

Where that heart on the refrigerator could remind him of all the reasons why it was okay to feel emotions. Because right now, he couldn't think of any. Not even one.

Saraia stuck a thumbtack into the picture of a mom with a tiny newborn in her arms. Beside her was her own smiling face as she'd stooped down to the woman's level to let Heidi snap a picture of them.

It was Janie and her new baby. She'd stopped by the clinic to drop off the picture in person, saying she'd left the baby with Jacob's mom in order to come, but she'd wanted to thank Saraia in person. Which she'd done, hugging her and telling her how grateful she was.

Sari smiled, touching the photo with her fingers. It was one picture in a sea of similar outcomes, so why did this delivery seem so special?

"Is that our dystocia patient?"

The low words from behind her made her whirl around, although she already knew who the voice belonged to.

Eoin stood there. This time, rather than faded jeans, he was dressed in khaki slacks and a blue button-down shirt. He looked cool and casual and especially yummy today, his perpetually disheveled hair pushed back from his forehead. A shiver went over her as her eyes tracked over him.

Was that why Janie's delivery had seemed extra important? Because he'd assisted her? If so, she'd better figure out a way to introduce a dose of reality to the memory. Because that delivery had been no more special than any other one had. She couldn't afford to let it be.

It didn't help that her girls had talked nonstop about the nice doctor they'd met a few days ago. The doctor who'd put together puzzles and colored with them.

Heidi had done a lot of that with them whenever she'd had to bring them to work. Evie and Hannah didn't think twice about that. Maybe because it was a normal part of the clinic. But let a handsome man come in and spend some time with them and it seemed to make an instant impact on them.

Well, he'd made an instant impact on her too. And she didn't like it. Because she was noticing far more about him than she should've: the way he looked, the craggy lines in his face when he smiled…the sound of his voice. And starting anything with him was out of the question. She'd done that with one other man, and it had ended up being a disaster. One that seemed to still be affecting Evie.

Sari realized Eoin was still waiting for an answer to his question. "Yes, that is Janie and Martha."

His eyes turned from her to the picture. "How are they doing?"

"Incredibly well, thanks to you. You just missed her by a few minutes. She wanted me to express her gratitude to you."

His eyes turned a shade darker. "Well, you win some, you lose some."

Shock spiked through her system. What an extremely weird thing to say. *"Excuse me?"* She couldn't keep the incredulity out of her voice—along with a hint of anger over how blasé and completely inappropriate his words seemed.

So much for an instant attraction. This was exactly why she didn't let men close.

"Oh, hell, Saraia—I don't mean that," Eoin said. "It's just been a shitty day, and seeing Janie's happy face just hit me in the gut."

She looked at him closer, and all of her anger melted when she saw what looked like a pinpoint of pain in his eyes. She touched his hand. "Hey, did something happen?"

He dragged a hand though his hair, mussing it even more. Her finger itched to smooth it back into place, to ease the line that had formed between his brows.

"I helped deliver a dead baby today."

You win some, you lose some.

Those words took on a horrible and sad new meaning. "Oh, Eoin, I'm so sorry. Do you want to talk about it?" Her fingers twined around his, seeking to somehow comfort him, but was that even possible? She couldn't even imagine what he was going through.

"Yes. No. Dammit, I don't know," he said. "You talked about my job and how specialized it is. I hadn't really even thought about it that way. I just know that by the time I'm called in, the odds aren't looking quite as rosy as they are when you step into a delivery room here at Grandview." He glanced at her. "And I'm not trying to minimize what you do, I just want you to know—hell, I don't even know what I'm trying to say. Do you want to get some coffee?"

She frowned, letting go of his hand when a little voice inside of her whispered that she shouldn't risk it, that she'd told herself over and over that she was immune to the charms of the opposite sex. But this wasn't about being charmed by him. Eoin was hurting, and to brush him off would seem callous. No, it would *be* callous.

Besides, he'd invited her to *coffee*. Not a wedding. And he needed to talk. And honestly, she wanted to help—or to at least be a listening ear. Wasn't she called on to do that with the women she served over the course of their pregnancies? This was really no different.

"Of course," Sari told him. "There's a coffee shop right around the corner. That way I can get back in less than two minutes if a patient comes in."

"Do you have someone scheduled for today?"

She blinked, then smiled. "My patients aren't always as predictable—time wise—as yours might be."

"I didn't mean that. I meant as in prenatal appointments."

Of course he did. "That makes sense. Sorry. And no, I don't have any appointments until later anyway."

"No kiddos with you today?"

She tensed slightly at the mention of her daughters. "Nope, they're in preschool. They don't get off until four, when I have to pick them up."

"I thought maybe they were in kindergarten already."

"This next year. They're excited but sad about leaving some of their friends behind."

He nodded. "I imagine it's sad to leave anyone behind."

"It is." It had been incredibly hard to leave David in the past, to realize that while she could hold his memory in her heart, she couldn't stay back there with him. For her daughters' sake she'd had to remain among the living, no matter how much she might want to wallow in the pain. To surround herself with memories of what they'd had and mourn him forever.

Leaving Max behind had been easier for her, since they'd not been together for that long. It had been harder for the twins. He'd been the only man they'd grown to know, not that they'd really known *him* in any meaningful way. They'd only seen the nice side of Max. The funny side, the tender side. But the man who'd mentioned wanting to leave his options open had been a total stranger. Sari thought back on that moment with a shiver. Talk about callous...

Her girls had seen the rosy picture, whereas Sari had been forced to face the reality. The cold, hard facts. That she and the girls hadn't meant nearly as much to him as she'd thought. And then trying to explain to them that he was never coming back... It had been hard. It was why Evie still got emotional even six months after the breakup.

Had it only been six months? It seemed so much longer. But now was not the time to dwell on that, especially since she'd agreed to go to coffee with Eoin. But at least her daughters would be nowhere around this time. If she ever dated again, she would leave Evie and Hannah out of the equation until she was very sure of the person she was seeing. That had been her biggest mistake with Max. But she wasn't that naive any longer.

Was she sure of that?

Ten minutes later they were in a quaint coffee shop that offered a choice of tables, either on the sidewalk, reminiscent of a French café, or in a covered patio around back. That was what she'd chosen, maybe because she hadn't wanted to risk anyone she knew passing by and seeing her there with him.

Not that she knew all that many people. Sari tended to keep to herself more than she had when David had been alive. He'd been an extrovert, never meeting a stranger. He'd been funny and charming and so very good at making people feel special. Whether it was her or some stranger off the street. Sari had always joked that without him, she'd probably wind up a hermit.

Except she hadn't. Their daughters had prevented her from hiding in a cave somewhere, mourning his loss forever. And surprisingly, she'd met some great people along the way. And she now worked with some amazing women who were as passionate about midwifery as she was.

Stirring creamer into her coffee, she looked at the doctor across from her. "I don't know how you do what you do, Eoin."

"How I do what?"

"Treat people who don't have happy outcomes."

His brows went up. "You can't guarantee those outcomes for anyone. Even at Grandview."

"True. I guess I should have said *people who are in crisis*. Do you lose a patient every day?" Once she'd said the words, she realized how cold they might have sounded. Those women were people, dealing with very real losses. But she didn't know how to take back the question.

"Not every day, no," he said. "But enough that it's hard to walk into that operating room when you're pretty sure it's not going to be a win/win situation, when you're faced with a molar pregnancy or birth defects that are incompatible with life."

She'd never faced a molar pregnancy before, where instead of a placenta, the egg and sperm produced a mass of fluid-filled cysts.

If there was an embryo in there, it couldn't survive. Sari couldn't imagine going to a doctor after having a positive pregnancy test, only to learn that not only were you *not* having a baby but that if you didn't get treatment immediately, you could very well die.

"What made you want to go into that field?"

"Obstetrics?"

"Not that so much. But taking on risky pregnancies."

"I don't know, really. Once I learned I couldn't…" He shook his head. "I think I liked the idea that I might be able to take something where the odds seem insurmountable and prove the world wrong."

"Except you can't always do that, can you?" She knew that well enough with her husband, who had remained in a coma for almost three weeks before finally succumbing to multiple-organ failure from an illness that had turned into sepsis. She'd prayed that, no matter what the doctors had said, he might beat the odds. But he hadn't. And it didn't give her a lot of faith in trying to win anything when the odds were stacked against her. Like fighting for her relationship with Max?

No, that had been an unwinnable situation. Like the ones Eoin said he faced on a daily basis. And fighting for someone who had no interest in staying? It would have only prolonged the inevitable and ended in disaster for everyone. Including Max. Including her children.

"No. You can't," Eoin said.

"And you don't regret choosing to specialize in at-risk pregnancies?" she asked. "Would you go back and change where you practice if you could?"

"There are times when I wish I had." He seemed to think for a minute before continuing. "But then there's that one baby who pulls through against all odds. Or that mom on life support that fights her way back to her family."

David had tried to fight, early on. Until the illness had consumed everything in its path. Wow, why was she thinking so much about this all of a sudden? The twins had been just three months old when he'd died. They had no memory of their dad outside of pictures, and to them that was all they were. Just images that had no real meaning to their young eyes.

Sari mulled over Eoin's response. "And

having one win for every twenty patients makes it worthwhile?"

He gave her a slight smile. "No. Not always. Not today. But tomorrow I might have a different answer. And that's what I have to keep thinking. That there are days when it really is worth it. Those are what keep me holding on, that keep me from throwing in the towel and walking away from it all."

"And those are the people who need you. *Really* need you." Her words were soft. She wasn't thinking of those critical patients, she was thinking of Janie. Janie, who hadn't been so much on the verge of death as she had been on the verge of losing it emotionally. Then Eoin had entered the picture with his soft words and calm manner and had brought her back from the brink and given her the strength to keep on trying, to roll onto her knees and trust what he'd said. It might not have seemed like much to anyone else, but to that patient it had meant everything. And she had a healthy baby to show for it.

"Sometimes I wonder."

Sari reached out and touched his hand. "Don't. Don't wonder. Believe it. You made a huge difference to Janie. And sometimes those 'wins' keep us going even when things seem bleak. When the going is so tough you're not sure you can go on one more day."

Was she talking to herself or to him?

Whatever it was, it must have resonated because his fingers captured hers and squeezed tight. "I needed to hear that today," he said. "More than you think."

His thumb trailed across the top of her hand, making tiny flames dance along her nerve endings. For several seconds she didn't move. Couldn't think.

Her eyes sought his and found that the blue was swirling with darker undertones that seemed to capture her. Draw her in.

Sari hadn't felt this strange sense of inevitability in a long, long time.

She only knew that she didn't want to move her hand away from his. Several seconds went by, and when she blinked they were both closer than they'd been seconds earlier.

How had that happened? If she leaned in another couple of inches she could very gently put her lips—

"Saraia Jones?"

The loud voice that came from somewhere over her head made her jerk back in her seat.

She looked up, halfway expecting to see a fiery figure emerge from the heavens asking what exactly she thought she was doing. But the only figure was a young man in an apron bearing the logo Grounded by Joe, the name of the coffee shop, whose owner was coincidentally named… Joe.

"Yes, I'm Saraia Jones."

"You're needed back at some birthing center." The man's glance went to her midsection as if expecting to see some kind of sign of pregnancy. Her face burned, especially after what she'd just been thinking about.

She reached in her pocket to feel for her phone, but there was nothing there. Oh God, what had she done with it?

"Okay, thank you. I'll go right now." Her glance went to Eoin, who was now sitting back in his seat, an inscrutable expression on his face. No sign of what she'd thought she'd seen in his eyes seconds earlier.

God! She'd probably imagined the whole thing. The burning in her face grew until she was sure it would burst into flames. Sari jerked her hand away and lurched to her feet, hoping beyond hope that she wouldn't have to walk beside him all the way back to Grandview.

"I'll follow you back in a few minutes." His voice was as cool as it had ever been.

Okay, well, evidently he was not as anxious to remain in her company as she was to stay in his. And somehow that was even worse because all she could hear was Max's voice as he'd said he'd wanted them to keep their options open.

"All right, sounds good." Maybe it really had been God telling her to wake the hell up. She'd known the man less than a week, and she was pretty sure if he'd tried to kiss her, she would have been a more than enthusiastic participant. And that scared her on a deeper level. Because it had been *her* who had been thinking of kissing him.

Thank God that hadn't happened. She didn't see how she'd be able to face him again if he'd reeled back in shock and dismay. Instead she reeled back—in dismay at her thoughts a few minutes ago.

Somehow she was able to walk out of the coffee shop on legs that were shaking—almost as much as her confidence in her ability to maintain a celibate lifestyle. Because the moment he'd stroked her hand, the moment he'd given her that look…celibacy had been the furthest thing from her mind.

Had she been crazy to think he'd felt the same thing?

But sex and relationships weren't synonymous, right? If she slept with a man, she wasn't bound to him for life—or until he wanted more options—right? Maybe she'd been looking at this thing all wrong. Max had been a pretty good vaccine when it came to repeating the same mistakes.

So what if she slept with someone? Maybe it would even be good for her.

Oh, no. It would not be good—if she was thinking in terms of Eoin. Oh, it might be *good* as far as the sex went. She was pretty sure it would be, in fact. But for some reason she was almost certain she'd have a hard time keeping her heart out of it if she went that route, and she wasn't sure why that was.

Because he was an attractive man? Maybe. Because she'd seen a vulnerable side to him that she hadn't expected to see when he'd talked about losing that baby? Yes, that was exactly it. His pain had been evident, if only for a few brief seconds. But it had been long enough that she was going to have a hard time banishing it from her thoughts.

But if she couldn't separate the two, then she had no business thinking about him in any way other than as a work colleague. She certainly shouldn't be imagining having sex with the man. She had a feeling he was no more interested in being in a relationship than she was. Although maybe he was already in one.

With the way his thumb had trailed over her skin? Not hardly. She might not have known him well, but she sensed he was not someone who would step out on a wife or girlfriend.

While that should have given her some comfort, it didn't. Because a taken Eoin was a whole lot safer than an available one.

The sudden spring in her step put paid to any such thoughts. Because the man *had* touched her. And that meant she might not have been imagining those molten glances he'd sent her way. And for some reason, it gave her a boost of confidence that had been lacking ever since Max had walked out of her life.

And that couldn't be a bad thing. Yes, she

was going to choose to look at it in a positive light. A man like Eoin might've been attracted to her. And she was attracted to him. As long as she didn't do anything about it, she could at least enjoy the fantasy of it. And boy, that fantasy promised to be almost as good as the reality of it. A very sexy reality if looks were any indication.

A few minutes later when she entered Grandview, Heidi caught her inside. "I've been trying to call your cell. So has the school."

"School? I thought I had my phone with me, but it must be in my jacket. Wait. Did you say school?"

"Yes. It's Evie," Heidi said. "The preschool tried to reach you, and when they couldn't they called here. She fell off some playground equipment and bumped her head pretty hard. They've taken her to the hospital."

"To the hospital?" Sheer panic gripped Sari, and she could only repeat the words back to her friend.

In a daze she realized Eoin had come in during the last part of their conversation. "Come on. I'll take you." He glanced at Heidi. "Which hospital?"

"Portland Lakes."

She heard the words. They clanged through her head again and again. Evie had fallen. Her baby. And now she was at Portland.

Oh, God! Please not again.

Minutes later, she was in Eoin's car and they were headed to the hospital where he worked.

By the time they arrived, more than her legs were shaking.

Was God punishing her for her earlier thoughts?

Stop it, Sari! she told herself. *None of that is important. The only thing that matters is Evie.*

Eoin pulled up to the emergency entrance and told her to go in while he parked the car. This was what it would've been like if David were still alive. He would've told her what to do and stood beside her.

But this wasn't David. And she didn't need anyone to stand with her. She'd been doing this alone for a very long time. With that thought in mind, she clicked off her seat belt, opened the door and, without a backward glance, got out of the car.

CHAPTER FOUR

SARAIA'S FACE WAS closed off by the time Eoin got inside. No sign of the fear or uncertainty that he'd seen back at Grandview.

"How is she?" he asked.

"I don't know. They said she's undergoing an MRI. A doctor is supposed to be out any minute to talk to me."

An MRI. This wasn't just a little bump on the head, then. "I'll wait with you," he said.

"You don't have to." Her words were quiet, but there was a flicker across the still planes of her face that he recognized from countless numbers of his patients. Fear.

There was no way he was going to let her go through this alone. Except maybe there was someone else she wanted here.

"It's okay—I want to." Well, he might not have wanted to, but he sure as hell was not going to leave her here by herself. "Is there someone I can call? A significant other? Evie's father?"

She gave him this look. This strange, pained expression that made him feel like he had missed something important. Knowing him, he probably had.

"Her father is dead," she said. "He died in this very hospital."

Shock held Eoin still for a minute, then formed a ball of unexpected emotion that he forced himself to swallow down. He'd assumed she was divorced.

"I'm sorry, Sari—I had no idea." He gripped her hand. "Come sit down."

He'd lagged behind her at the coffee shop because her words about people needing him had whispered to a place deep inside of him that he'd thought he'd cemented shut after breaking up with Lucy. He'd looked at Sari, and suddenly all he'd wanted to do was tug her toward himself. And do what? Kiss her?

He wasn't sure.

When that employee had come up and told her she was needed at the clinic, whatever spell that had been woven around them had broken, and he'd been glad she'd been called away. *Glad!*

And that probably damned him to a very special place in hell.

They sat in hard plastic chairs that were easy to sanitize but did nothing to provide any comfort to families waiting to hear news of any kind.

Like Saraia when she'd gotten the news that the twins' father had died?

He wrapped his arm around her in an attempt to do what the chairs could not. And she leaned her head against his shoulder for a second before popping up to look at him in panic. "I need to call my mother-in-law and ask her to pick up Hannah. And I don't know where my phone…"

"Use mine." The man who'd died had not only been the twins' father but Sari's husband.

Eoin placed his phone into her palm and watched as she stared at it before covering her mouth with her hand, tears dripping down her cheeks. "I can't… I don't know…"

He got it. In this day and age of just pressing a button, most people had stopped memorizing phone numbers. He took the phone back and called Grandview.

Heidi picked up immediately. "How is she?"

"No word yet," he said, "but Sari doesn't have her phone with her. Is there any way you have her list of emergency contacts there on the computer?"

"Yes, of course. Is she wanting to call Peggy?"

"Is that her mother-in-law?"

"Yes. Wait just a second…" Heidi's voice came back a second later. "Here it is…"

She rattled off a series of numbers that he typed into his phone. "Got it—thanks."

He pressed Call and handed the phone to Sari, who clutched it and put it to her ear.

A second later, she said, "No, it's me, Sari. I don't have my phone with me."

She glanced at him before continuing. "I'm okay, but Evie's been hurt. I'm at Portland Lakes. Is there any way you can pick up Hannah from preschool and take her home with you?"

Evidently Peggy said something because Sari quickly added, "No, please, just take her home. I'll call you as soon as I know something. She'll just be scared if she comes here."

Something else was said, then Sari relaxed in her seat, giving Eoin a slight smile. "Thank you so much. I'll call as soon as I know something. She's being examined right now."

She pressed the End button and handed the phone back to him. "Thanks for coming in with me."

"Not a problem." But he didn't put his arm back around her, nor did she attempt to put her head back onto his shoulder. But even without that, he felt this weird connection that he couldn't remember feeling before. Was this what it would be like to have a wife? A family?

That yearly letter slid back through his mind, and he quickly dismissed it.

Sari wasn't his wife and Evie wasn't his daughter. Even when he'd been with Lucy, he hadn't given thought to wondering about what it might be like to have children with her. Until she had started pushing. And Eoin hadn't liked the future he'd seen between them.

He wasn't sure why he was even thinking about Sari and fatherhood all of a sudden. Whatever it was, he'd better nip those thoughts in the bud before they started growing. He'd been in a vulnerable place this morning, and Sari had talked him through it. He was pretty sure that was what this was all about.

But Sari was just a colleague. A temporary one at that—because he wouldn't be at Grandview forever. Although he hadn't set a termination date on the volunteer form, he'd somehow had it in his mind that this gig would last a year at most. Until Grandview could find someone more permanent. Any physician at the birthing center would have little more than a desk job, as it didn't sound like emergencies came up all that often. And Eoin couldn't see himself doing something like that long term.

Like Sari had said, people at Portland Lakes needed him. And in all honestly, he probably needed them too, despite the heartache that all too often came with the job.

Dr. Sidle, one of the pediatric neurosurgeons at the hospital, came out. He shook hands with him, a question in the man's eyes that made Eoin tense, then he turned to Sari. "Are you Evie's mom?"

"I am. How is she?"

"We suspect a concussion, but there's no immediate evidence of a brain bleed. She's over in imaging just to make sure. And we'll want to keep her for the night just as a precaution after a fall like that. She has a pretty big goose egg on the back of her head."

Sari's eyes closed before looking at Eoin again. "I can't thank you enough for bringing me or for letting me use your phone…"

"Don't mention it." She didn't realize it, but she'd just given Sidle a plausible explanation for their being together.

Plausible? Hell, it was actually the real explanation. There was no "plausible" about it.

Sidle looked at him again, and Eoin felt the need to say, "Sari is a midwife at Grandview, where I'm volunteering."

"I see. Good thing you were there," Sidle said. He didn't ask why she hadn't driven herself here in her own car or why she didn't have her cell phone with her. And if he knew the neurosurgeon, he wouldn't ask later either. They were colleagues but not drinking buddies. And right now, Eoin was glad of it.

"When can I see her?" Sari asked.

"It'll be about a half hour or so," he said. "Once they're finished doing the MRI, we'll get her in a room. As soon as that happens, one of the nurses will come out and get you."

She stood and held out her hand. "Thank you so much."

When the doctor left, she dropped back in her seat, and Eoin said, "I'm so glad she's okay."

"Me too. I'm sorry for snapping at you when you asked about her dad. I just… When I heard she was here, my brain stopped working. I was so afraid."

"I get it," he said. "Do you want to call Peggy and tell her?"

"I need to go back and get my phone and my purse, and…"

He shook his head. "No, you don't. I'll drive back to Grandview and get them. Do you want a ride home?"

"I'll probably stay the night until she's discharged. Peggy will come and get me when we're ready." She leaned over and kissed his cheek. "Thank you for everything."

She didn't know it, but somehow she just had. That kiss made him feel warm and tight and…what was it that she'd said at the coffee shop? Needed. He'd felt needed in a way that went beyond the hospital walls.

"Do you want to go for a walk? It might be good for you to get some fresh air," he said.

"We won't go far, and I can give the nurse's station my number if they get her in a room sooner than expected."

"That would be wonderful," Sari said. "I don't know how to repay you for bringing me here. I'm not sure I was capable of driving."

"No repayment necessary. Do you want to call your mother-in-law before we go?"

"Yes—thanks."

When she ended the call, Eoin was more than ready to go out and get a breath or two of fresh air. Anything other than sit here and think about what could have happened with Evie, what could have happened between him and Sari in that coffee shop.

And yet he was about to go on a walk with her? It was just a walk.

They found themselves in the large courtyard that lay between the wings of the hospital. Two magnolias stretched high overhead providing shade to the benches below. They wouldn't bloom for several more months, but they were still beautiful.

"Do you want to walk?" Eoin asked. "Or sit?"

"Could we walk, please?" she said. "I'm not

sure sitting still out here would be any better than being in the hospital."

"Of course."

A stone pathway wound its way between flower beds that were awash with color, and before Eoin could think of something to say, Sari glanced up at him. "I can't imagine losing one of my girls, I'm not sure I could…" Her voice trailed away.

Was this what being a parent would be like? That clawing fear of losing someone. He'd seen his own parents overcome with emotion more times than he cared to remember when he'd been going through his own treatments. Eoin had carried such guilt over putting them through everything, and yet he knew it hadn't been his fault. They'd told him that every time they'd had to rush to the hospital and he'd whispered how sorry he was. In the end, it had bound them closer together, and although they now lived in Florida, they talked on the phone at least once a week and his parents traveled to Charleston most Christmases.

He reached down and gripped Sari's hand. "She's going to be fine—you heard the doctor."

"I know," she said. "The thoughts just race through my head, and I can't seem to stop them. Maybe I pushed them too hard to try new things, to be adventurous. Maybe I—"

Threading his fingers through hers, Eoin gave her a soft squeeze. "Stop. It was an accident. Nothing you did caused this. Kids get hurt, no matter how hard you try to shield them."

This time, she smiled up at him. "Thanks. And a lot of it is just the fear of the unknown."

"I get it," he said. "I'm not a parent, but I've seen it with my own folks."

"I think we all must go through that. I'm pretty sure even after we grow up, our parents don't lose that fear."

Eoin wasn't a parent and might never be one. It was something he was careful not to talk about with his own mom and dad. He was sure they would've loved to be grandparents, but unlike Lucy they'd never asked about his banked sperm or what he intended to do. At this point, they'd probably given up hope of him actually becoming a father.

"I'm sure when you're a single parent it's even harder," Eoin continued. "How long ago did you lose him?"

He didn't say who he was talking about, and he wasn't sure why he'd even brought it up, other than the shock of hearing that she'd lost her husband.

"David died when the girls were just three months old," she said.

"And you've been doing this alone ever since."

Sari looked up at him, her eyes soft. "Sometimes. But it's surprising how often people step up to help, even when they don't know about David."

Was she talking about him? Hell, he hadn't done anything other than bring her to the hospital. But he had stayed, even when a voice inside of him had been telling him to leave.

Because of what had happened in the coffee shop?

Yes. It would have just been a kiss. Nothing more than what she'd given him on the cheek in the hospital.

Seriously? Because what he'd wanted to do went way beyond that. Way beyond the meeting of two sets of lips. And that scared the hell out of him.

"There are a lot of people who care about

you, from what I've seen," he said. "Heidi. The other midwives. Your mother-in-law."

He left out himself because even the thought of including himself in that contingent was enough to make him want to turn around and walk away. But how could you meet someone like Sari and not care about her? He'd cared about plenty of his patients. All of them, if he really sat down and thought about it.

And maybe this was part of the reason he'd been drawn to her. Maybe he'd sensed something in her that said there was more to her than the cool, competent midwife he'd seen his first day at Grandview.

"I know a lot of good people," she said.

"Yes, you do."

They walked in silence for several more minutes before she stopped and faced him, letting go of his hand. "I just want to say thank-you. Not just for now, but for coming to Grandview, even when you weren't so sure about us."

He smiled. "I wasn't. But I think you're in the process of convincing me."

"Am I?"

There it was again. That softness that beckoned him to move closer to her, to take her into his arms and hold her close. But he wasn't going to. Not because of her words that he knew had been said half in jest, but because of how those words made him feel. Like he wanted her to convince him of a lot of other things. Things he had no business thinking about. Especially at a time like then when Sari's daughter lay in a hospital bed.

So he tried to put some mental separation between them. "All of you are," he said. "And you should be proud of the work you all do at Grandview."

She gave a slight frown. "We are. It's a great team."

This time she didn't say how glad she was that Eoin was part of that team, and he was glad. He needed to put a little distance between his emotions and Sari. Because they were becoming a little too convoluted.

Or did he mean complicated?

It didn't matter. All he knew was that he did not need to put himself in a position where he would have a hard time letting go when the time came. And he had a feeling it might prove a little more difficult than he wanted to believe.

So he needed to make a conscious effort to keep things professional, to keep his work life and his personal life separate before he—

His phone buzzed, and he looked down at it. It was the number to the hospital. "Hello?"

He glanced at Sari as the nurse relayed the message that Evie was now in a room and she could go see her. "Okay, thanks."

"Evie's all set. She's in room 321."

She nodded. "Thank you again, for staying with me. I really do appreciate it. But I'm good."

"Are you sure?"

"I am," she said. "And Peggy will come get me in the morning."

"Okay, I'll run back to Grandview and get your phone," Eoin offered. "Please tell Evie I said hi."

She didn't respond, but then again he hadn't expected her to. Maybe by the time he got back, he'd be able to get his head together and stop thinking thoughts that shouldn't even be on the horizon. At least not on his horizon.

Eoin came back with Sari's purse and her phone about a half hour later, but instead of coming up to the room, he'd thankfully waited for her at the nurse's station. And when she got there, he barely said ten words to her beyond asking how Evie was doing and if Sari was sure they didn't need a ride when she got discharged.

When she said she had it all figured out, he left it at that and headed up the elevator of the hospital, probably going to wherever his office was located. Compared to the behemoth that was Portland Lakes, Grandview was a tiny speck on the map when it came to hospitals and clinics.

Sari remembered the feeling of being lost when David had been here. She could never seem to locate his room, and when she had, the sheer number of machines keeping him alive had boggled her mind.

In the end, they hadn't kept him alive, though. His body had been weary and so, so sick, and it had finally signaled that it had been done fighting. She'd been one of the fortunate ones who hadn't needed to decide when enough was enough. His heart had stopped in the middle of the night, in spite of the work of the ventilator, in spite of the crazy number of tubes and IVs huddled around his bed.

She remembered squeezing his hand and telling him that she loved him before she'd sent him off to whatever the next step had been in his journey. His babies had been right there beside her, the way they'd been for all those days and nights of uncertainty.

At least she wasn't sending one of her daughters off to that unknown place. Evie was okay. She'd been lucky, everyone told Sari. Yes, she had been. But so had Hannah and Sari and Peggy. To lose someone else would have been unimaginable.

One thing she wasn't going to do was tell Evie that Eoin had said hi. She didn't want to see a sheen of excitement in her girl's eyes over a man ever again. At least not one who was only in their lives temporarily and as nothing more than her work colleague.

By the time she got back to Evie's room, her daughter was awake, hands going to the big white bandage around her head. When her daughter smiled at her, Sari lost it, tears she'd been holding back for the last hour pouring from her eyes.

"Mommy? What's wrong?"

"I'm just so happy to see you, baby." She went to the chair beside the bed and perched in it as close as she could get to her daughter. "Does your head hurt a lot?"

"Not anymore. They gave me a shot with a needle that was this long..." Evie held her hands as far apart as they would go.

It was then that Sari truly believed her daughter would be okay. It was such an Evie thing to exaggerate and make a molehill into a Mount Everest.

"Where's Grammy and Hannah?" she asked.

"They're at home," Sari said. "But I'll call them and tell them how big that needle was."

"Aren't they coming to the hospital to see me?"

She gripped her daughter's hand. "I think it might scare Hannah and Grammy to see you in here." She didn't want to say that Peggy might have a hard time facing this hospital after losing her son here, even after all these years. "But they'll come pick us up tomorrow morning, okay? Hannah is excited that she'll have to miss a day of preschool. And if you're up to it, we'll get some ice cream on the way home."

Evie drew a deep breath and let it out in a

sigh before yawning. "Can I have the chocolate swirlie thing?"

"Of course. It's what you always get." She drew her daughter's hand to her mouth and kissed it. "You get some rest, and I'll be right here when you wake up, okay?"

"Okay. I love you, Mommy."

Out of the corner of Sari's eyes, something moved in the doorway. She turned to look and was just in time to see someone turning away from the room and walking away.

She could have sworn from the hair that it had been Eoin, but she'd been sure from the way he'd left her standing at the nurse's desk that he'd been on his way somewhere else. Maybe it hadn't been him, maybe it had been someone who'd simply had the wrong room. But she replayed the scene in her head over and over again as her daughter slept in the bed beside her chair. If it had been Eoin, maybe he simply hadn't wanted to interrupt them.

In the end it didn't matter who it had been. Because Evie was alive and she was safe. And Sari wouldn't take that for granted ever again.

Eoin couldn't get the picture of Sari kissing her daughter's hand out of his head. He'd gone up to his office, then on impulse had descended back to where the pediatrics wing was located and stopped by the room to check in and see how things were going. He'd been just in time to see the emotional scene. His eyes had burned, and he'd turned away, deciding then had not been a good time to stop in for a chat. Or anything else. Because the scene had threatened to draw him in, to make him a part of it when he wasn't.

The shock of learning that Sari's husband had died at Eoin's hospital had nearly unraveled him, especially after finding out how young his daughters had been. Eoin could only imagine how it felt for her to walk back through those doors. But she'd done it. Not that she'd had a choice.

The fact that she loved her daughters fiercely had never been more obvious. And raising them alone? People did it all the time, so why was this any different?

Eoin didn't know. All he knew was that when he'd stood in that doorway, he'd wanted to help her in some way. A way that went far beyond just walking with her in the hospital courtyard. He'd wanted to relieve her of a tiny amount of her burden. But why? He knew her from work.

It's called compassion, Mulvey. Nothing more.

A couple of hours went by before he got up the courage to go back to the room and look in on them. He'd hoped to find Sari asleep in the chair, but no such luck. The second he appeared in the doorway, she turned to look, her mouth forming an O shape as if surprised by something.

"It was you before."

The whispered words barely reached him.

Hell, so she had seen him. Had she seen his reaction too? He hoped not.

He kept his voice low so as not to wake Evie up. The quiet snoring sounds from her bed made him smile and wonder if Evie's mother sounded like that too. He quickly shook the thought off. "I did peek in earlier just to see if you needed anything," he said, "but you were talking, and I didn't want to disturb you guys. She's still doing okay?"

Sari shook her head, her smile big and wondrous. "She's… Evie. I've never been so happy to hear someone laugh."

"I can imagine." And he could. Not as a parent, but he'd witnessed his own mom and dad's heartache when he'd been diagnosed and treated for his cancer. And he'd witnessed other people's pain, had seen it in Sari's eyes when she'd told him that Evie's father was dead. "Is there anything you need?"

"No. Are you not working today?"

"I have some paperwork to do. Nothing that can't wait." It was a little white lie, but he somehow didn't want to leave the hospital knowing she was sitting in vigil beside her daughter's bed, so he'd put it off.

"Do you want to…sit with us for a while?"

He hadn't expected the question. In fact, he wasn't quite sure Sari had meant to ask it, wasn't quite sure how to answer. He went back to his earlier thoughts about wanting to relieve her of a tiny bit of her burden.

She quickly said, "You don't have to. Please don't feel—"

The strain in her voice made up his mind. "No, of course I'll sit with you. Like I said, I don't have anything pressing right now." He doubted anyone would, since they'd expected him to be long home by now. He didn't want to leave. But he wasn't sure how smart it was to stay. "Do you want me to bring you a coffee?"

"That would be wonderful—thank you."

"Cream and sugar, right?"

Her brows went up as if surprised. "Yes."

"I'll be right back."

Taking the elevator to his office, where his coffee maker was, Eoin made two cups of coffee, adding cream and sugar to hers and leaving his black. While going through the motions, he quickly worked out two things. First of all, he was doing something any colleague might do: sit with a friend who was going through a hard time. And secondly, he wasn't sure he was cut out to be a father. Oh, bringing kids into the world, he was all about that. But he always handed them off to someone else to care for. To find out your child could have died during an accident on the playground?

Judging from his visceral reaction to seeing Evie lying on that bed—a girl he'd only met one time in his life—he could only imagine what he would have done had she been his. He'd have broken down completely.

Was that so wrong? He thought for a minute. Maybe not for someone else, but Eoin had always kept a tight rein on his emotions. He'd learned to as he'd gone through his treatment for cancer. He'd always felt he had to be strong for his mom and dad. He'd smiled his way through chemo, even while inside he'd been so terrified that he was going to die. When he'd been so sick he could barely lift his head but had somehow managed to do just that so that he wouldn't scare his parents.

Which was why when he'd lost that baby this morning and then had to talk about it with Sari, he'd felt a vulnerability he didn't often show to the world. It felt alien—almost wrong, somehow. And then right on the heels of that he'd heard about Evie's accident and watched as Sari had cried silent tears over her daughter's bed. It was too hard.

Other people could evidently cope with letting their feelings out, but he couldn't. Because he'd always been the strong one.

And having a kid? He was certain his facade would crack and fall off in chunks, leaving the real him exposed to the world. He was pretty sure that moms and dads had to be even stronger than he'd been as a young man who'd been faced with his own mortality. He'd kept it together. Then. For his family.

Locking those thoughts behind the door of his office, Eoin headed back down the elevator with both mugs in his hands. When he reached the door of Evie's room again, he went through and started to hand Sari her coffee before stopping mid reach. Her head was thrown back against the chair, her hand still clutching her daughter's. But her eyes were closed, and there, in soft quiet tones, were the echoes of her daughter's snuffling snores. Only they weren't from Evie this time.

He smiled, and the weight and heaviness of his thoughts seemed to fall away as he sat back down in his seat and enjoyed the guilty pleasure of listening to them both. Like mother, like daughter. He was sure that Sari would be horrified to know he'd just discovered the answer to one of his questions. Saraia Jones, midwife extraordinaire, did indeed snore.

Eoin was gone when Sari woke up to sunlight pouring into the window of Evie's hospital room. In fact, she couldn't remember him coming back with her coffee, for which she was mortified. There was no sign of the coffee or of him. But he'd left a simple note, and she smiled when she read it.

Call if you need something. I'll be around. E.M.

And that was it. But it was enough. She appreciated everything he'd done during her crisis. Although hopefully he hadn't stuck around and watched her sleep because she was pretty sure her mouth had been hanging wide open when she'd woken up.

And Evie had a roaring headache today but still wanted the ice cream Sari had promised her. Her daughter seemed no worse for wear, otherwise, after her tumble off the playground equipment. And the doctors said after two or three days she could go back to preschool, which had surprised Sari. For some reason she'd thought it would be longer…or maybe she'd just hoped to be able to sit with her daughter at home and prove to herself that Evie really was okay.

At that moment, Peggy peeked in the room followed by Hannah. "How are we doing?"

Hannah rushed over to hug her, clinging to her hand, while Evie squealed.

"Grammy! Mom said we could go get some ice cream, 'cause of the fact my head hurts."

Sari's mother-in-law gave her a quick look that spoke of worry.

She shook her head. "Just a headache. The tests don't indicate anything other than a mild concussion. They said her head would probably hurt for the next day or two."

"Thank God."

"About the ice cream. You don't have to—"

"Nonsense," Peggy went over and kissed Evie's head. "If my granddaughter wants ice cream, ice cream she'll get."

That made Sari smile. David's mother had been so wonderful to them, even though the girls had to be a constant reminder that she'd lost her son. But on the other hand, they were all that remained of David. And while she could have been clinging and controlling, she never had been. She'd been a source of wisdom when Sari had asked for advice. But she'd also never pushed her opinion onto Sari, for which she was grateful.

"Okay, but we won't stay long."

Peggy smiled and gave her a quick hug. "We'll take as long as you need."

Raw emotion swept over Sari and her eyes

prickled in warning, but somehow she kept the tears from spilling over. But her voice did break as she said thank-you.

Fortunately, her mother-in-law acted like she hadn't even heard it. She just helped her gather her daughter's paperwork and held her hand out for Hannah, while Evie clutched her mom's hand.

They chose a shop about twenty minutes from the hospital and one of her daughters' favorite ice cream places. Stepping out of the car, the humidity of Charleston encased them in a moist hug that wouldn't let go. Going into the air-conditioned shop was a relief.

Located not too far from one of the local beaches, Beverly's Cream and Gelato boasted white clapboard siding. Colorful caladiums and flowers spilled from two window boxes that flanked a white door, and café-style tables sat on the sidewalk for those willing to brave the heat of the day. Today, Sari was thankful for the tables that lined the walls inside the establishment.

They ordered sundaes for the girls, and Sari got a simple vanilla milkshake. Peggy opted for her favorite blackberry gelato. Finding their seats, they slid into the booths with the girls in the inside.

Peggy reached across and squeezed Sari's hand. "She's going to be okay, you know. I'm just sorry you were there by yourself until this morning. I would have come up last night."

"Eoin stayed with me until Evie was settled into her room," she said.

Hearing her name, her daughter piped up. "I didn't get to say goodbye to him."

Sari smiled. "Because you were asleep, silly."

But something in her regretted that she hadn't been awake when he'd returned with her coffee. Because she, too, would have liked to have said goodbye.

"Eoin…?" Peggy asked.

"The doctor that Grandview hired."

"I remember you telling me about him. But I think you used his title."

Sari felt her face flush, even though there was no reason to feel guilty. Peggy had heard her call all of her colleagues by their first names plenty of times.

"I probably did."

Her mother-in-law's head tilted, and she

studied her for a moment. "Well, I'm glad he was there for you."

Evie spoke up. "He colored with us at the clinic. He's super nice."

"Super nice," Hannah repeated.

"Yes, he is." Sari's face heated even more. Why did it sound like they were all infatuated with him? She wasn't. At all.

And that little scene at the coffee shop?

What scene? Nothing had happened. Nor was it likely to. She'd simply felt badly for what had happened to his patient.

Really, Sari?

Yes, really.

"I can tell." Peggy gave a quick laugh. "You need to get out more, Sari. In some ways I feel like you closed yourself off after everything that happened with…" She lowered her voice to a whisper and leaned closer. "Max."

Sari glanced sharply at Evie to make sure she hadn't heard. But her daughter was happily chattering with Hannah about the hospital and the "tube" ride she'd had to go in.

"Can you blame me? I have them to worry about." She tilted her head toward the girls to indicate who she was talking about. "I have one who is still grieving that loss."

She immediately regretted her choice of words, since Peggy carried a grief even greater than the loss of a relationship. She'd lost her son. Sari squeezed the fingers that still gripped hers. "I'm sorry. That didn't come out the way I wanted it to."

"Oh, honey, it's okay," Peggy said. "And more than anything, David would want you to be happy. It might not have happened with that last…guy. But some day the right one will come along."

Sari wasn't so sure. She no longer allowed herself to think along those lines. Not because of David, who Peggy was right about. He wouldn't want her to hold on to his memory and stop living. And realistically, she couldn't. She had his daughters to raise.

"Well, so far he hasn't," she said. "So I'm not going to worry about anything other than getting Evie home and making sure she's okay."

"Please don't let what I said upset you." Peggy glanced past her. "And it looks like they may be about ready."

"I'm not upset. I'm grateful for you each and every day." Sari gave her a smile that she hoped took any sting out of her earlier words.

She knew Peggy meant well and that the self-lessness that it took to want her daughter-in-law to be happy with someone other than her son was probably a rare quality. One that she treasured.

They left the shop, and the ride home was filled with talk that had nothing to do with relationships and everything to do with the girls and their preschool activities. Sari tried to relax in her seat, but a thought kept breaking through.

What would Peggy think if she knew that Sari had almost kissed a man she barely knew? She'd probably be ecstatic, since as she'd said, David wouldn't want her to sit around and mourn him forever. Although sometimes Sari thought that might be the wisest course. Dating Max and then breaking up with him hadn't been the easiest thing to do, and there was no guarantee that the same thing wouldn't happen the next time and the next and the next. And then there was Evie's response to Max walking away from them. She'd been traumatized for months.

But Sari wasn't going to worry about any of that. She was going to go back to work tomorrow, and on Eoin's next day at the clinic, she was going to treat him like a colleague and nothing more. She was pretty sure he didn't want more than that either. Yes, they'd held hands after he'd shared with her about the loss of that preemie during the cesarean section. And again in the hospital courtyard. They'd each been hurting, although for different reasons. People often turned to someone for support during difficult times, didn't they? It was also the reason she'd asked him to sit with them when Evie had lain in that hospital bed. So they'd both reached out to whoever had been nearby for comfort. It had just happened to be each other.

It was an easy enough thing to understand and didn't mean anything. Which was a relief. Because despite her earlier thoughts about sex, the last thing she needed was a messy fling or anything else from someone who she wasn't even sure shared her values about midwifery and natural childbirth.

So with that thought in mind, she was going to concentrate on getting home, where she could put all of her foolish thoughts to rest once and for all. From here on out, she was going to jump back onto the train of professionalism—and make sure that train clung to the tracks like its life depended on it.

CHAPTER FIVE

SARI HADN'T CALLED HIM. He hadn't really expected her to, and a part of him was glad. And yet he'd wanted to know how Evie was doing. Her daughters had gotten under his skin. They were cute and outgoing and weren't afraid to speak their minds. They reminded him of their mama.

He'd had a few days to think about their interactions, both at the café and later at the hospital. He decided to chalk it up to the stress they'd both been under. It was probably a normal thing when you started working with someone attractive to wonder what they were like in other ways.

Other ways? Seriously, Mulvey, are you twelve?

And then to learn that her husband had died at Portland Lakes had been a blow. The temptation had been there to ask someone about it, but that would be violating HIPAA rules. Besides, it was none of his business. None.

So, after some deliberation, he decided to do…nothing. And today he was due in the clinic in a half hour. More and more he was thinking that volunteering there had been a mistake.

No, not a mistake. Maybe he'd needed this time in a labor-and-delivery center where patients were screened to avoid as many surprises as he encountered. For a while now he'd felt like his job involved running headlong into a hurricane and doing his best to snatch people out alive. And when he finished one day, he woke up the next and did it all over again.

At the birthing center, he could slow down and maybe enjoy the process. If they let him into the room. That had been a shock to find out that they wanted more of a desk jockey than a real doctor. But maybe they'd made that clear to his hospital administrator and the man hadn't relayed their expectations. Although Eoin had been glad to be there for Janie's delivery.

Walking through the clinic doors, he spotted Heidi and Saraia along with another woman who was wearing scrubs that sported tiny diapers all over them. They were all looking down at something. Heidi and the other woman both looked up when he drew near and smiled.

The woman in scrubs came over to him and held out her hand. He grasped it and let go.

"You must be Dr. Mulvey. I'm Miranda Brady. Sorry I haven't gotten to greet you yet. I ended up helping with a home birth your first day here that took longer than expected and didn't make it in. I heard you helped Sari with Janie Magee's delivery, though. Thanks for that."

Evidently here at Grandview they were a little looser with patient information. Although since it was a much smaller, more specialized clinic, the midwives probably saw most of the patients at some point or other.

"I have no doubt that Saraia would have handled it just fine, had I not been here," Eoin said.

Miranda tilted her head. "Sari thinks differently—said you swooped in and saved the day."

This time Saraia's head popped up, eyes wide. "I didn't quite put it like that."

The other midwife laughed. "It's called dramatic license, Sari. Anyway, she said you were a 'big help.'" She surrounded the last two words with air quotes and turned and eyed the other woman. "Better?"

Color flared in Saraia's cheeks, something he'd noticed happened whenever she seemed flustered. He liked that characteristic. And the way her silky dark hair accentuated her delicate features.

Her twins had her dark hair as well.

And why was he even thinking about that? Time to move to a different subject. "How's she doing? Janie, that is."

Okay, now it sounded like he was avoiding asking about Evie, and that wasn't what he'd wanted. He'd meant to come in and ask Saraia about it right away but had gotten sidetracked.

"Did you see the picture she brought in?" Miranda went over to their huge corkboard and pointed to the snapshot. "They're doing great. And she got in with her pediatrician for an early appointment this morning and let us know that there was no sign of nerve damage from the shoulder dystocia."

"Good to hear." This time he looked at Sari, who was looking everywhere but at him. She seemed as ill at ease as he did. But he had to push through it, or this arrangement was not going to work. "How is Evie doing?"

"She's fine. My mother-in-law is keeping them home today, just in case, even though the doctor cleared her to go back to pre-school."

"Already?" Eoin's brows went up, but he wasn't about to question the pediatrician's advice. "I'm sure she'll enjoy her day with Peggy."

Miranda's eyes swiveled back to him. "You've met Peggy?"

This time Heidi piped up. "Sari went to the hospital and forgot her phone, so she had to call her using Eoin's phone."

"Dr. Mulvey was there with you? At the hospital?"

"Call me Eoin—everyone does." He smiled. "I offered to take her since she had no idea how badly injured her daughter was."

Saraia dragged fingers through her hair, and he watched it sift back into place, every lock looking soft and touchable. "I was in shock. And Heidi needed to stay here at the clinic."

"I get it," Miranda said. "At least now. Sari just left out a whole swath of the story."

Had she? Why? It wasn't like they'd been on a date or anything. It had been an emergency situation. Eoin decided another change of subject was a good idea.

"What were you looking at when I came in?"

Miranda turned a sheet of paper to face him. "Our schedule for the week. We normally have patient appointments on Monday through Thursday. Fridays we try to keep the schedule a little lighter so we can rotate Fridays off and each get a long weekend once a month." She fixed him with a glance. "Have you sat in on any appointments yet?"

"No, not yet." He shot Sari a look. Which she deftly avoided.

"Dr. Eric didn't sit in on appointments," Miranda said, "but he'd been here for a few years. I'm sure he probably did initially to see how we handled things."

Saraia spoke up. "I did mention doing that for the first couple of weeks. But it kind of slipped my mind since we normally do them on our own." She glanced his way. "Sorry about that."

He gave her a slow smile. Somehow he didn't think she'd forgotten. She'd been pretty prickly about her patients that first day. But he thought he could see why. Maybe some ob-gyns would come in and try to take charge, since it was what they normally did at the hospital. They had the last say in almost everything. Which was different from how things worked here. And maybe that was a good thing. Maybe these patients didn't need an authority figure stepping in for a few minutes and then leaving until it was time to catch the baby. Maybe these women wanted more of a partner and found that in these midwives.

"We can check with our patients, to be sure, but the majority should be fine with having you in there. If that's something you want to do," Miranda said. "Dr. Eric knew how things ran and chose to sit out appointments. It's a system that worked for us. But if you come on board for longer you'll have to decide what part you want to play in the clinic. I can almost guarantee it's not as exciting as your current position."

Saraia was now watching him with interest. Maybe trying to see how he was digesting this new information from Miranda. And as far as staying for longer than he'd agreed for? The jury was still out on that.

But he had just gotten done thinking that volunteering at Grandview might be just what he needed. A kind of counterbalance for what he did the rest of the week. "I agreed to do whatever needed doing here. But yes, I would be interested in sitting in on at least a few appointments."

"Well, take a look at the schedule. The first couple of patients are Saraia's. So as long as she and the patient are good with you being there, then I say go for it."

Sari gave a strained smile. "Of course I am. When they check in, I'll ask them and then call you in."

"That sounds good to me."

Miranda pointed to three appointments in the afternoon. "And I'm pretty sure my patients will be fine with your presence as well."

"And the ones later in the week?"

Sari came around to look. "Those are Kat's patients. You haven't met her yet since she's normally only here on those days. She does the bulk of our home births and sees most of her patients there."

"So there are three of you in all?" He thought he remembered Sari giving him a number, but things were a bit foggy about that first meeting. So much had happened since then.

Heidi spoke up. "Five, really. A couple are on-call midwives who come in as they can. Normally on their days off from their other jobs." She punched a couple of keys on the computer at the desk and turned the screen toward him. A spreadsheet came into view with color coding. "Each color represents one of our on-call midwives and their availability."

Okay, wow. They did quite a juggling act here. "And this system works well?"

Sari laughed. "Not always. But so far it's done a pretty good job of keeping us straight. There are weeks when everyone wants to be born at once and weeks where we feel we are twiddling our thumbs, but both of those extremes would be the exception to the rule. It's normally pretty steady. And speaking of steady, here comes our first patient."

The three women scattered, leaving Eoin standing at the desk by himself. He was pretty sure he hadn't been hired as a greeter, so he went back to the micro-office they'd given to him. At six by six, the space was definitely small. Just big enough for a desk which took up half the space and two chairs, one on either side of it. There was no computer. Nothing at all in it except for those three items of furniture. There weren't even any pictures on the walls. He couldn't hide a smile. It was as if they didn't want their resident doctor to get too comfortable. But he got it. He wasn't the important figure when it came to the clinic. It was these midwives who supported their patients both physically and emotionally. They were the ones who took center stage. And from what he could see, they did an admirable job of it.

Eoin took his cell phone out of his pocket and placed it onto the desk. He halfway wondered if Sari would even call him in for her appointments. She'd told the truth and had made the offer, but she hadn't seemed very eager to have him in there with her when they'd spoken on that first day. But he got it. She was probably a little bit suspicious of his profession, given her own personal experience with one giving birth. But just like every midwife was different, so was every doctor. They each had their own quirks and preferences. It was what made them human. But most of them truly cared for their patients and wanted the best for them.

His phone buzzed. He punched answer and then put it up to his ear. "Hello?"

"If you want to step in, I'm in exam room one." The phone went dead. Okay, it was Sari's voice, though she still didn't sound overly thrilled. But he would take her invitation at face value. At least she'd asked the patient. She could have just ignored him and left him sitting in his cubicle.

He headed for the exam room, then knocked, waiting for a response.

When he got one, he slid into the room, closing the door behind him.

Sari glanced over at him. "Mabel, this is Dr. Mulvey. He's the obstetrician who's partnering with the clinic at the moment."

Eoin smiled at the woman. "Nice to meet you. I'm just here to observe, if that's okay."

"Yep, fine with me."

Sari went through the motions, doing a lot of what happened in the hospital. The difference was she did a lot more conversing about life and families than he might have done had he been the one in charge of this exam. But he was pretty sure that was what these women were here for.

"Charles is working today, so he couldn't make it," Mabel said. "But he's already asked off for my next appointment. After all, the baby is getting close."

Watching as Sari measured the woman's belly, he would guess she was at eight month's gestation. "I bet he's excited."

"He is. We all are."

Eoin took up a post toward the back of the room, since he was only here as an observer.

"The baby's still active?"

"Yes." Mabel rubbed her belly. "She's wants to be a soccer player, from the way she's kicking."

So this woman had opted to know the sex of her baby, unlike Janie.

"Oops! There she goes again."

Saraia laughed. "I saw that one. It looks like she's moved into the head-down position already. She's getting ready. Did you get the nursery done? I know you said Charles was working on it the last time you were here."

"He still is. But she'll be staying in our

room for a bit to make it easier, so we still have some time yet."

"Yes, you do." She reached out a helping hand, and Mabel grasped it, sitting upright. "It looks like everything is on track. Baby is a good size, but not overly so. So next month we'll switch to every week so we can track the changes in your cervix and get a better idea of when she might want to put in an appearance."

"Thank you. At this point, I'm ready for it to be over."

Sari smiled. "I get it, but not much longer."

The woman slid off the table and put her flip-flops back on, glancing at him. "It was nice to meet you, Doctor. Thanks for being our 'just in case.'"

Okay, well, it was the first time he'd been called that. By anyone.

But he got what she'd meant. After all it was why he'd banked some of his sperm—just in case. And most of the women who walked through the clinic wouldn't need his services. Just like he might never use what he'd saved. It was why that letter came year after year. As a reminder that it was there.

Just in case.

Sari walked Mabel out to the front, and Eoin stood there for a minute staring at the table. Maybe it was time to check a box on his "just in case" letter and make the decision he'd been putting off. If he ever did decide to have a child, there were other ways of doing that. Adoption, for one. Would it limit his prospects as far as partners went? Maybe, but this was his choice to make. Not theirs.

Going over to the table, he started the cleanup process, stripping the paper off and discarding it. He found a spray bottle of sanitizer and spritzed the table and wiped it down before pulling a fresh strip of paper over the table.

"Hey, what are you doing?" Sari asked.

He stopped before turning around. "I thought I could at least do this, if nothing else."

She frowned. "We don't expect you to clean exam rooms."

"So, you have a cleaning crew to do it or a nurse's aide?" He softened the words with a smile.

"Well…no. But…"

"So that leaves who? You?"

She smiled back. "Well, yes. But I'm a woman of many talents."

"So I've seen." It was better not to elaborate on those words, so he simply added, "It's kind of nice to have a break from my normal day, so if you're okay with it, I'll pitch in where I can."

"Does that include washing windows?"

He was pretty sure she was joking, but to be safe he gave an honest answer. "If needed."

"I'm not quite sure if you're being serious or not." She said it in a dubious way, as if she expected there to be a catch. But there wasn't one. And what he'd said was absolutely true—it was nice to have a break from his frenetic schedule. The atmosphere here at the clinic gave itself to that. It had a calm soothing presence, and Eoin couldn't quite put a finger on the reason for that. Maybe it was the midwives who worked here.

If so, he could only hope some of it rubbed off on him and that he could carry it with him through the rest of his week. He was scheduled to deliver a hydrocephalic baby on Wednesday, which promised to be a tricky affair as the neonate would need surgery as soon as it was born.

It. He hadn't asked the sex of the baby. Hadn't even wondered if the parents knew. And maybe that was a failing on his part. He did think of his tiny patients as people. But he wondered if it was his way of remaining aloof and doing his best not to let them touch any deeper than his skin, which was pretty damned thick. Except for that baby last week—the one who'd somehow reached inside of him and yanked at a part of him that he hadn't been sure still existed.

Evidently it did. And he wasn't sure that was a good thing.

He glanced at Sari, who was still standing there. "I'm very serious. I really do want to help, you know. I didn't come here to change the way you do things. Maybe you can even teach this old dog new tricks."

"Old dog. Hardly." Her nose squinshed in a way that was pretty damned adorable.

"Try living in my skin for a day."

She sighed. "I get it, believe me. There are days when we all feel like it. The trick is just to keep going until the feeling passes."

Sari had more reason than most to feel world weary and tired. She'd lost her husband and, from what Eoin could surmise, was raising her twins without help from anyone but Peggy. And yet she still felt genuine empathy for her patients and their babies. She still managed to get through the days when she felt unsteady. He had done his best to bolster her on the one day he'd seen her struggle. When Evie had been hurt.

He took a deep breath and let it out. She'd ended up bolstering him earlier that same day, when he'd been emotionally shaky after losing his patient.

"I really am glad that Evie is okay," he said.

"Me too. It could have been so much worse."

Something flashed in her eyes that said she knew exactly how much worse it could be. Her husband had died in the hospital. So yeah. She did know.

"Was it hard being at the hospital?"

He immediately regretted asking the question. Of course it had been.

"So very hard," she said. "I told Peggy to stay in the car so that she wouldn't have to face coming in when Evie was discharged. And I didn't want Hannah in there. But of course, Peggy wouldn't hear of it and insisted on coming up to help us get down to the car. She's a strong woman. Far stronger than I am."

Shock rolled through him. There was no way those girls would even have any memory of him. That had to be hard too. "Hell, I'm sorry, Sari," he said. "I can't imagine what it was like to go through something like that."

It was true, even though he'd gone through a pretty tough time himself when he'd been eighteen.

"It was pretty terrible. David picked up an infection from somewhere and turned septic. He was in a coma for a few weeks and never woke up from it."

From what Eoin remembered, the twins had only been three months old at the time. So there she'd been with two infants while her husband had been dying from an illness that hadn't responded to treatment. Portland Lakes was a world-class hospital, so if they couldn't figure it out it was doubtful anyone could have.

"Were you already a nurse midwife at the time?" he asked.

Sari leaned against the wall, head tipped back. "I was already a nurse. But I decided to go back and study midwifery because of how uncomfortable I was with my own birth experience. I ended up getting my doctorate-in-nursing degree." She glanced at him. "So why'd you go into obstetrics?"

That was trickier because it meant going back to his cancer diagnosis and the possibility that he'd never have biological children. It wasn't something he wanted to revisit. Not right now. "You know, it just felt right when I was going through school. All through my rotations I had this idea that obstetrics was where I would end up. And it was." It sounded so simple when he said it in those terms. And in a way it was. It was as if he'd been born to be in this profession. And if he'd never had cancer? That was a question he couldn't answer because his life experiences weren't something he could make disappear.

"Yes, it was. And from what I can tell, your patients are very lucky." She paused. "And I think we are too."

Something warmed in Eoin's chest. He'd had people compliment him before, but coming from someone who had been so prickly toward him at first? It meant a lot. A whole lot. If he wasn't careful, he was going to get stuck in an emotional quicksand that he'd have a hard time escaping. So time to get busy doing something. Anything.

He forced a smile. "You're just saying that to be nice."

"When have you ever known me to just be nice?" She rolled her eyes, and her nose crinkled again. It was just as cute the second time. "Wait—don't answer that."

"You can be nice. When you want to."

This time she laughed. "I thought I told you not to answer that."

Just like that the seriousness of the moment disappeared and they were in lighter territory. And Eoin found himself enjoying the back and forth between them, wishing it could go on a little longer.

So he lobbed her earlier words back at her. "When have you ever known me to do what I'm told to do?"

"Touché, Dr. Mulvey."

He reached and gave her hand a light squeeze before releasing it. "When is your next appointment?"

"In about twenty minutes. Do you want to sit in again?"

He found he wanted to, especially with how open to the idea she seemed to be. It was light-years from the way they'd started off their relationship. Strike that—it wasn't a relationship. But he found he liked being with her, liked watching her work. "If it's okay with you," he said.

Sari tilted her head and studied him for a second before smiling again. "Sure. It's a first-time mom, and this is her first visit, so it'll be a lot lengthier than the last appointment."

"It's fine."

"Sounds good." She glanced around the room. "And since you've so expertly prepped this room, we'll see her in here. After all, I'd hate for all of your hard work to go to waste."

Yep. He definitely liked being with her. And that should've sent up a warning flag in his head. But it didn't. At least not one that he was willing to acknowledge. Instead, he'd just take today for what it was: A chance to learn a little more about what she did. And why she did it.

Eoin had surprised her, and that wasn't easy to do. When Sari had gone into that exam room, she'd been prepared to clean the room herself before her next patient arrived. But to see him wiping down the table had been somewhat of a shock. Dr. Eric had certainly never offered to do any of those things. But then again, he'd been close to retirement and it had probably never crossed his mind to clean exam rooms since he didn't sit in on appointments.

And for Eoin to joke about it had made her heart lighten. It had been a while since she'd been able to joke with someone of the opposite sex.

She hadn't even joked that much with Max—which, looking back on their relationship, didn't seem normal. And she certainly hadn't with Dr. Eric, who'd, in her mind, been kind of an Eeyore figure. In fact, he was the one who'd asked them to call him Dr. Eric, since that's what he'd had his patients call him.

In the time Sari had been at the clinic, the former obstetrician only been pressed into action a handful of times. In fact if the crisis with Janie had happened during the time when Eric Reynolds had been here, she probably would have bypassed him and called one of the other midwives for assistance. It was just the way they did things. She wasn't even sure why she'd called Eoin in, but it had worked. He'd surprised her there too by not continuing to take charge once the emergency had been over.

Her respect for the matter-of-fact way he was able to laugh at himself grew as they waited for their next patient—who came sailing into the room with her husband at that very moment. Cassidy was all smiles over the wonder of their impending entry into parenthood. They were newlyweds who'd wanted to have children right away and who, it looked like, had hit the jackpot. Unlike Sari, who'd had trouble getting pregnant while married to David and had opted to see a fertility specialist. It hadn't been a fun time, and her fluctuating hormones had turned her into something of a monster. In the end, when the process had consumed them and started to affect their relationship, she'd opted to discontinue treatment and surprisingly had gotten pregnant with Evie and Hannah six months later.

She greeted the pair. "Hello, I'm Saraia Jones, and this is Dr. Mulvey. He is our clinic's new resident doctor. Do you mind if he sits in on this first visit? He's getting on track with how we operate."

They looked at each other, and then Cassidy shrugged. "It's okay with me. We'll still have natural childbirth, right?"

"Absolutely—if everything checks out okay for that," she said. "The next couple of appointments we'll be doing a lot of measuring and tracking and I'll be asking a lot of questions, just to make sure you have the safest delivery possible. So let's get started, shall we?"

Eoin stood at the back of the room as Sari took Cassidy's weight and measurements and asked a barrage of questions about the couple's medical and familial histories. No inherited problems from what they said, no history of twins on either side of the family. And Cassidy's pelvis was wide enough to accommodate an average-sized baby, from what Sari could determine.

"I'd like to do a transvaginal ultrasound, if you're okay with that. I want to see where baby implanted and see if we can hear any signs of a heartbeat."

"A heartbeat?" Cassidy looked at her husband. "I didn't even expect to hear that today."

"Well, there are no guarantees," she said. "But since you think you're closer to eight weeks pregnant, we might be able to sneak up on the little one and coax a preview."

She prepped the patient for the procedure and told them what to expect, then rolled the machine over and set the parameters on the screen. Then she introduced the wand and searched for the baby. It didn't take long. "There. The baby has implanted nice and high in the uterus, which is what we like to see." She nodded at the monitor.

Sari clicked on either end of the fetus, measuring its length. Within normal ranges for a pregnancy of eight weeks. Then she heard it. The thready *bub-bub-bub* that signaled the beginnings of cardiac activity.

"Is that...?" Cassidy's voice contained awe and a little bit of surprise.

"Yes, it is. Your baby's heartbeat."

The new mom grabbed her husband's hand. "Oh, Brett..." Her voice choked up, and she couldn't say anything else.

When Sari looked over at Eoin, she noted that he was staring down at his feet. In boredom? This must've seemed pretty blasé to someone who had heart-stopping cases that kept him on his toes. But when he glanced up, she swore that there was something in his face other than indifference. It looked more like what she'd seen in her patient's expression. He looked away so fast, though, that she wasn't even sure what it was that she'd seen.

Turning her attention back to her patient, she finished up the exam and printed off a copy of the sonogram before pulling the curtain back around the pair so Cassidy could get cleaned up and dressed. She had already done a tour of the facility and stated her dream was to have a water birth. Sari had confirmed that was still their goal. And if everything she'd seen today held steady Cassidy might very well have her chance to have that. They still needed to see the blood and urine results that they'd send the pair to get.

Once they came out, Sari asked if they had any questions, and when there were none, she sent them out to Heidi's desk to get scheduled for her next exam in a couple of weeks' time.

Then she turned to Eoin. "So what did you think?"

"It was…something."

She frowned. That was a weird response. "I'm not sure what that means."

"By the time a pregnancy arrives on my doorstep, no one is smiling and I'm facing a

set of very worried parents. And a whole lot
of questions—some that I can't answer. To be
on this side of things and to see such… Well,
happiness is a change for me."

"It's a nice change, though, right?"

His mouth canted up on one side. "I want
to think so. But a big part of me is waiting
for the other shoe to drop. For something to
go wrong. It's so ingrained in my DNA as a
doctor who sees at-risk patients at every turn
that it's hard for me to believe that 'normal'
will stay that way. Even your shoulder-dys-
tocia patient had a few minutes when things
could have gone badly—"

"But they didn't. And at Grandview 'normal,' as you put it, happens the vast majority
of the time."

That sexy line in his cheek deepened. "Will
it make you mad if I say I have to see it to
believe it?"

"Mad? No. Because I hope you'll see the
things that I've seen each and every day of
my career. A sense of happiness and expec-
tancy in my patients that makes me love coming to work." She took a step closer. "I get
that it's unnerving for you, but we're serving
up joy and light here at Grandview, so don't

bring any of your 'anti-joy' into my exam room, okay?"

"Anti-joy?" His brows shot up.

She'd meant it as a joke but realized it could have come across as super insensitive since he dealt with the opposite side of the spectrum in his practice. "Sorry—I phrased that badly."

"I get it. And truly, I try not to bring any of that to my own cases. In fact, I strive to bring hope to some pretty heartbreaking cases, but it's not always possible." He gave a half shrug. "But I'll try to make sure I'm happiness and light personified when I'm here."

Happiness and light personified. She wasn't sure she would ever describe him as that. There was an air of broodiness and... yes, sadness to the man, but she could also believe that he would try to find hope in the hardest of situations, and she had to respect him for that.

"Glad to hear it," Sari said. "Now, I don't know about you, but my stomach is growling. Are you up for some lunch?"

"I am. Where did you have in mind?"

"I'll tell you. But first we're going to put

your newfound skills to work and get this room prepped for the next patient."

He gave her what could be a fake scowl. At least she hoped it was fake.

"Happiness and light personified, remember?" he said. "Happiness and light."

When laughter bubbled up from somewhere deep inside her, she couldn't stop it from coming out. "Just keep on saying that, Eoin, and everything will be fine."

CHAPTER SIX

TRAVOLI'S WAS A little Italian eatery just off Charleston's famed Broad Street. Within sight of the crisp white steeple from St. Michael's Church, the area was both beautiful and crowded, bustling with tourists who loved to shop along the palm-tree-lined street. The wait hadn't been long, but the line behind them was growing by the minute. It was good that Sari had suggested arriving a little earlier than noon.

"Have you ever been here before?" she asked.

"No, this is a little hike from Portland Lakes. I normally just try to grab something from the hospital cafeteria."

She made a face. "Ouch. Well, once you eat here you may never go back to your normal routine again. It's a little distance from Grandview too, so I don't usually take my lunch breaks here. But it's great for a treat. Evie and Hannah love it here too."

"Well, then, it must be good. Did you hear from Peggy? How is Evie doing?"

"She's good. They're already begging to be allowed to spend the night. Grandma spoils them."

Eoin couldn't hold back a smile. "I can't blame her. They're a pretty cute pair. At least they were when I saw them last week."

"Thanks. They can be a handful, but I love them more than anything."

What would it be like to have little human beings that made you feel that way? From the little time he'd spent doing puzzles and coloring with the twins, it was easy to see how they could win your heart. They'd done a number on his. A few days ago, he'd been pretty sure he was going to opt not to save his sperm, but he was wavering. Again. Just like he did every year.

There was just such a permanence to the decision. Once he told them to destroy the samples, there would be no going back. The chemo all those years ago had destroyed any chance of him producing any more sperm. It was why he'd held on to the stored batch for so long, why he'd made no move to finalize things, even though he'd been wavering about the decision for the last five years. And if he did the same this year, it would make six. Six years of vacillating between two possible futures: one without kids, and one with.

But he hadn't wanted to have those kids with Lucy—that much was obvious. He'd thought the problem had been about fatherhood at the time, but looking back, it had been more than that. What had seemed so right when they'd met on a blind date, when they'd started dating in earnest had turned sour when she'd started in on how much Eoin would love it if they had a child together. And he'd never been quite sure why things had turned so bad so quickly, but they had. He'd never once looked back and wished things could have turned out differently. And breaking things off had been a relief.

And since Lucy was no longer in the picture, that left surrogacy or adoption as the only options. That would mean raising a child on his own, unless his relationship status changed anytime soon. And he didn't see that happening. He glanced at Sari and gave an internal shake of his head.

Don't get any ideas, Mulvey.

Once seated at their table, Eoin decided to forgo the wine menu since they were still working and had a soda instead. Sari did the same.

She opened her menu, and the light from a nearby window spilled through the locks of her dark hair, giving her an ethereal air that tugged at his heart. He caught himself studying her, admiring the way her brown eyes were intently perusing the options she found on the page in front of her.

"Mm…" Her teeth came down on a corner of her lip. "Okay, Eoin, what sounds good to you?"

His mouth suddenly went dry at the incredibly sexy sound she'd just made. At how she'd paired it with his name, making all kinds of things come to mind.

Things he should not have been thinking. Maybe it had just been too long since he'd been with someone in any meaningful way.

Yes, that had to be it. Except that weird attraction kept popping up when he least expected it to. Lurking just below the surface in the things Sari said. At the unexpected way she'd touched his hand when he'd been struggling to make sense of the loss of one of his patients.

He could admit there was some chemistry here. But working together brought far too many complications to risk venturing down that particular path.

Maybe he should try to meet other women. Although how to go about that when he rarely went anywhere except the hospital was a big question. He was normally too exhausted.

And yet right now he felt pretty energized. Because he was here with Sari?

Damn!

He forced himself to study the menu. "I think I may go with a simple chicken parmigiana."

"That does look good," Sari said. "I normally get the ravioli Florentine. Maybe I'd better stick with something I know I'll like."

And there it was again. The words that he could twist around at will and make into something that had an entirely different meaning.

Thank God their waiter came and took their orders, then brought their drinks. Eoin took a big swig of his, wishing he'd ordered beer or something stronger instead. If ever he'd needed a drink, it was now. But he never drank alcohol while working. And then there was the case of having no social life, so he rarely drank *ever*.

Maybe he really did need to make an effort to put himself out there. But he wasn't sure he even knew how after all this time. And telling someone about his cancer diagnosis and sperm-bank deposit seemed like a real mood killer.

"Mommy, Mommy!"

Sari's head came up in a flash and jerked to look toward the right. Two little rockets hurtled toward them, and she turned just in time to brace herself for their impact.

The girls planted kisses on their mother's face before one of them turned in his direction. "Oh, it's you! Yay! Do you still have your heart?"

It took him a second to realize what she was asking. Not about his literal heart but about the picture he'd colored. He nodded. "I still have it."

Sari shot him a look.

"I'll explain later."

The midwife glanced past the girls. "Where's Grammy?"

"She's picking up our food because we begged her to come here. But she said only if she could take it home. She said Evie still needed her rest."

So the speaker was Hannah. It would take a while for him to be able to tell them apart. Not that he had that kind of time. Because he wouldn't be seeing them on a regular basis. And strangely that made him feel a little bit weird inside. Because they were sweet and funny, and he could see how they would keep their mom on her toes.

"Does Grammy know where you are?" Sari asked.

Hannah glanced over her shoulder. "Yes. She saw you first and said we could come over."

As if summoned, Peggy appeared carrying a white plastic bag containing what was probably their lunch. She glanced at Eoin and her brows lifted slightly. "Sorry to interrupt your lunch, but they would have been devastated if they'd known you were here and didn't get a chance to come over."

"It's okay." Sari gave him a glance that had a wary look to it. The same look she'd given him when she'd found him coloring with the twins in the clinic lounge. Did she not trust him with them?

God, he hoped that wasn't the case. He wouldn't do anything to hurt either one of these kids. Wasn't it obvious by his profession that he loved children?

But he got it. In today's world it wasn't always easy to know who to trust around those who were so precious to you. Maybe he should talk to her about it.

And say what? That he wasn't the kind of horrible person that you heard about on the news?

He could say it, but how would she know, really?

So he decided to just let it go. He wouldn't be spending hours alone in their company anyway.

Sari motioned to him. "Mom, you remember Dr. Mulvey, don't you? He took me to the hospital after Evie's accident."

"Eoin, right? I do," Peggy said. "I'm glad you were there to help my granddaughter. She means the world to me."

He was surprised she knew his first name, but then of course Sari would have talked about her colleagues. He also liked the way she called her mother-in-law "Mom." But it seemed like something she would do…making those in her life feel important and loved. "I know she does. And I'm glad she's okay."

"Me too." She motioned to the twins. "Well, girls, we need to go and let Mom eat so she can get back to work. I assume you're not off yet."

Sari's face turned pink. "No, not off."

"Mom, Grammy said we could spend the night with her if it's okay with you. *Ple-e-e-ease?*" One of the twins broke in and saved them from having to explain further.

Sari glanced at Peggy. "Are you sure? You've had them all day already."

"I'm sure. I never get tired of having them around. I have extra clothes and pj's at the house." She stroked Hannah's hair, while her arm held Evie close to her side.

Yes, Eoin's parents would have loved to have grandkids. His heart tightened in his chest. If things ran true to course, they might never get that chance.

"Okay," Sari said. "I'll be by to pick them up for preschool in the morning."

"Sounds perfect. I'll make breakfast for all of us."

"Oh, you don't have to—"

Peggy made a shushing sound. "I want to. Please let me."

There was a tremulous quality to her voice that made his gut tighten. It was easy to forget that not only had Sari lost her husband but Peggy had lost her son as well. And from what he could see there wasn't a significant other in the older woman's life.

Sari reached out and grabbed her hand. "Thank you. You do so much for us."

"You're family." The simple words were said with a smile before Peggy gathered the twins together and hustled them back through the restaurant. One of the girls kept looking back and throwing kisses to her mom.

"They're adorable, you know." The words came before he could stop them.

She looked at him with a smile that made his heart cramp with some strange emotion. "Thank you. Like I said, they're my world."

Their waiter chose that time to come and set their artfully plated food in front of them. Soon the conversation turned back to work and their different fields, comparing notes on how they each did things.

Sari asked what his most memorable happy ending was.

Eoin told her, leaning forward as he remembered different aspects of a woman who'd come in expecting to hear that her baby had an inoperable problem with one of his kidneys, only to have Eoin share that he'd found a specialist who had treated a similar case in utero. And while he hadn't performed the actual surgery, he'd observed, and when it had come time to deliver the baby, she'd been healthy and strong, with no sign that there had been a problem at all, except for a small incision on her back that would fade with time.

"That's wonderful," Sari said. "I'm sure times like that make the harder cases a little easier to bear."

He thought for a minute about his last tragic case. "Maybe not easier, but if they were all hopeless, I might change my specialty. Maybe those sad cases make me celebrate the good outcomes a little more than I might otherwise."

She nodded. "I think I take things like that for granted—those good outcomes. But after meeting you… Well, maybe I won't do that anymore."

"You're blessed" was all he said before remembering that this woman had experienced her own share of heartache.

But if she'd had the same thought, she didn't let on. She just smiled and said, "I know it. I just need to look at life differently sometimes."

"I think we all do."

Her cell phone rang, and she checked it. "Oops—hold that thought. It's the clinic. Just give me a minute."

"Hi, Heidi. What's up?"

She listened for a few minutes before responding again. "Are you sure?"

The other woman said something else, and then Sari said, "Okay. Call me if you need me, then. I'll tell him."

She hung up and then shrugged. "Well, that's a first. My last appointment had to be rescheduled and the clinic has been slow today, so she said for us to take the rest of the day off. They'll call if something comes up."

Eoin chuckled. "Well, that's a first for me too. Not the part about a patient canceling, but I don't think my hospital has ever told me to take the rest of the day off."

"I mean, I have taken the day off before, but it's normally been something planned."

"Are you going to go pick up your kiddos?"

Sari bit her lip. "I think Peggy and the girls would all be disappointed. They normally eat and then curl up on the couch together watching movies for a few hours."

"Well, if you don't have anything pressing, I have an idea," he said.

"Obviously I don't, since I was expecting to be at work the rest of the afternoon. So what did you have in mind?"

Sari wasn't sure how, but they wound up at the end of Folly Beach Pier that stretched out over an expanse of blue ocean. Located on Folly Island, it was southwest of Charleston proper, and the pier along with the white stretch of beach that surrounded it was a popular spot for fishing and tourists alike.

"I haven't been here in ages," she said. "Not since they rebuilt the pier."

Folly Beach Pier's wood pilings had been heavily damaged by shipworms over the years. The decision had been made to close it for two years so that the pier could be reconstructed—this time with concrete support structures that would be impervious to marine worms.

Sari took a deep breath and turned her face toward the sea breeze, letting it whisper past her skin. "I'll have to bring the girls—they'll love it."

David had never been a fan of the ocean—or any bodies of water, really—since he couldn't swim. It was the one thing that they'd differed on. Standing out over water like this would have made his anxiety go through the roof. She'd had the girls in swimming lessons since they'd been old enough to walk for this very reason. They were little fish, loving every minute of their water time. She was pretty sure David would have approved, although it wasn't something they'd talked about during her pregnancy.

Eoin stood by the rail hip, propped against it as he faced her. They'd talked about work and about life in general—something she hadn't done with a man since Max. Since having a brief panic when she'd found the obstetrician coloring with her daughters the other day, she'd come to the conclusion that she was being silly. He was a work colleague, and Evie and Hannah had met plenty of her friends and colleagues over their lifetimes. She and Heidi often did stuff together with them and her own kids. She was like an aunt to them, since Sari had been an only child whose parents had died in a car accident years ago. Maybe Peggy was right—maybe she did need to allow more people into her life.

And Evie seemed to have turned a corner where Max was concerned. There'd been no more crying at school over his absence—something Sari was grateful for.

She glanced at Eoin, loving the way the stiff breeze ruffled his hair and plastered his denim shirt against his torso. Heidi had been right that first day about him being cute. But it went way beyond that. The man was downright gorgeous. From his blue eyes right down to his narrow hips. She was surprised he wasn't married or attached by now. And he wasn't. Or they wouldn't have had that moment at the café last week.

"So how did you know about Folly Pier? Did you grow up in Charleston?" she asked.

"Yes, born and raised here." He smiled. "I used to teach surfing lessons down on this beach while I was in college to help pay for my books."

Her brows went up, and she glanced down at the surrounding waves. "You surf? You know they found an alligator swimming in the water here several years ago."

He chuckled. "I heard about that. I haven't surfed in the last few years, though."

She somehow found that surprising and she wasn't sure why. Maybe she was comparing him to David. But she thought it was more than that. "My girls would probably love to do that someday. As you can tell from Evie's fall, they're kind of daredevils."

Sari wondered if that too wasn't because of their dad's fears. If maybe she hadn't pushed them to do things that he might have been afraid of. When the school had called about Evie's fall, Sari had poured herself a stiff dose of guilt, wondering if it had been partially her fault. But, like Eoin had said, kids fell, right? They got hurt, right? She couldn't wrap them in bubble wrap and coddle them.

What was with this sudden dissecting of her late husband? She and David had been happy enough, despite the water thing.

"I think I was surfing almost from the time I could walk."

Somehow the image of Eoin in diapers riding the waves made her laugh.

He tilted his head. "What?"

"It's nothing."

He reached over and touched her hand. "No, seriously, what? Is the idea of my surfing that ludicrous? It got me through some tough times."

What kind of tough times?

"No, of course not. I was just picturing you in diapers on a surfboard." She shrugged. "See? It was silly."

He smiled but didn't move his hand. "I'm sure I was potty trained at an early age."

"Oh, you were, were you?" she teased. "You remember that far back?"

"No. But I'll remember this," he said. "Thanks for coming out here with me. I needed this more than I realized."

"Did you? Because I think I did too."

The atmosphere on the pier slowly shifted as they looked at each other. Her laughter dried up, and something rose to take its place. The dozens of people milling around them faded to nothing as her glance dropped to his lips, her tongue moistening her own.

His fingers tightened on hers before someone bumped her from behind with a muttered apology. But it shuffled her closer to Eoin until she was just inches away from him. Where she swore she could see into his very soul. Those blue eyes glimmered with some kind of light from within, and she couldn't stop herself from staring into them.

"Eoin…"

His free hand went up to the hair at her nape and sifted through it, teasing out a tangle he found there. Then his fingers trailed over her cheeks, down the edge of her jawline. Sari caught her breath and held it, afraid to move. Afraid she would do something to sabotage whatever was happening here.

Everywhere he touched came alive as if she were being rebuilt from the ground up, just like the pier had been a few years ago.

She suddenly wanted him to kiss her with a desperation that left her shaky. She hadn't wanted something this much in… She couldn't remember when. She lifted her face toward him.

As if Eoin understood her silent plea, he closed the distance between them and canted his mouth across hers, a light touch that could barely be considered a kiss. But it set her on fire. She edged closer, going up onto tiptoe in an effort to reach him. Then his fingers tunneled deep into her hair and his mouth covered hers again, this time leaving no uncertainty that he wanted to do this.

And she loved it, kissed him back in a way that said she could give as good as she got. It was sexy, fun, and she wanted it to last forever.

But of course, it couldn't, and when Eoin eased back to look down at her, his palms cupped her face. She braced herself for an apology or some kind of rational explanation for what had happened. Except his gaze contained a heat that found its equal inside of her.

"I want so much more of that."

The low words were nothing like the ones she'd expected him to say, and she relaxed into his embrace.

"Me too."

"Do you?"

When she nodded, he leaned down to kiss her again. "But not here. Not where everyone can see us."

She knew what he was asking. And it wasn't about kissing. It was about so much more. Without hesitation, she traced the line in his cheek and nodded. "Let's go, then."

"My place?" he said. "It's just a few blocks from here."

Somehow she managed to get the word "Okay" out. She couldn't believe she was doing this, couldn't believe she was about to go back to Eoin's place. Sari wasn't an impulsive person. Or...at least not anymore. When she'd been younger, yes, absolutely. But after David's death and later the breakup with Max, she'd become a more sober person, thinking through each and every decision she made.

But this felt good. It wasn't hurting anyone, and for once she was going to do something wild and impetuous...something just for her and her own pleasure.

At least she hoped that was what Eoin was planning. If he just wanted to sit and talk, she was going to be sorely disappointed.

But when he dropped another searing kiss onto her mouth, she knew it had nothing to do with talking and everything to do with action.

The return trip down the pier seemed to take forever as he towed her behind him, steering around people who were out fishing or just gathered together in groups. Sari vaguely wondered how many other people had been bewitched by the beauty of the pier and had made the same trek back to their houses to make love.

Make love?

You could call it that, even when there was no love involved, right? This time it wasn't about a relationship. It was about pure need. Unadulterated craving.

She realized she'd been sizing him up for this since that first day in the clinic, although she would have been mortified if anyone had noticed. Especially Eoin. But he hadn't. At least she'd seen nothing in his demeanor that said he'd witnessed her surreptitious glances.

He loaded her into the car and finally let go of her hand long enough to go around to his side. Since his vehicle had manual transmission, he had to work the stick shift in the heavy beach traffic. But there was something about the way his fingers slid over the mechanism that made her think about how his hands would soon be sliding over her body. It made her shiver.

He must have noticed because he fiddled with the climate-control knobs. Except her reaction had nothing to do with being cold and everything to do with the heat that was sliding over her, a heat that was tightening her nipples while softening other parts of her body. In preparation…

God! If the clinic called now, she was going to scream in frustration.

She just wouldn't answer the phone.

No, of course she would. Because that wasn't who she was. She might say that she was going to take this for herself, but it was hard to remember a time when she hadn't had so many responsibilities weighing down on her.

Her job. Her girls…

No! Don't think about that now, she told herself. *Just enjoy the fact that a handsome man wants you. And you want him back.*

She did. So very, very much. "How much further?"

She hadn't meant to say the words out loud, had meant them to be trapped with the other dialogue that was singing inside her head.

Eoin glanced at her and smiled. "Just a few more blocks. I promise." He reached over and squeezed her hand until he reached another intersection.

Then they were pulling into the lot of an apartment building a few miles from the beach.

"Wow, you must love living this close to the ocean," Sari said.

The building was painted in a sea-washed blue that looked perfect in this setting.

"I don't go as often as you might think."

He parked and came around to let her out of the car. Keys in hand, he walked up a flight of stairs to the second floor. He opened the door and let her walk in ahead of him before closing it behind them.

She could feel his eyes on her as she took in the space. It didn't have the dark leather sofa and huge television screen that she would expect in a bachelor pad. Instead, the furnishings were light and airy and perfect for a beach retreat. And it was neat. Really neat. As if this wasn't where his life happened.

"No TV?" she asked.

"There's one in the bedroom." He took her hand and tugged her toward him. "And no, we're not going to watch it."

She smiled and leaned into him, the scent of ocean air still clinging to his clothes. And his hair was a wreck. A very sexy wreck. She reached up to twirl a lock around her finger. "I would be very disappointed if you said we were. I might even have to wrestle the remote out of your hand."

"I might like to see that, actually." His arm wrapped around her waist and held her against him, where she could feel every hard line. "Not the remote part. But you and me… wrestling on the bed."

Sari would definitely like to experience that. Lots and lots of wrestling.

This time when Eoin kissed her, he kept her pinned to his body and squirmed to get nearer. She loved his masculinity and confidence. Because she needed this, needed to be swept away by someone in a way that hadn't happened in a long time. Max had been all about the sex in the beginning of their relationship, but as time had gone on and the girls had become more involved in their lives, he'd spent more time in front of the television than anything. And she wondered if it had been because he hadn't wanted a ready-made family.

Not something she should've been thinking about right now. Not when she was being kissed by a sexy man in the living room of his house.

He lifted his head. "Do you want a drink?"

Of him? Absolutely. Of anything else? "No."

"In that case…" He swept her up into his arms and carried her down a short hallway to a bedroom. This one was masculine, with a bed that had dark heavy posts and looked like it could withstand any amount of wrestling. "We have to be quiet, though. I have an eighty-nine-year-old woman living in the apartment below mine who might be scandalized."

Sari's brow shot up, and he laughed. "I'm kidding. I'm assured that the soundproofing in these apartments is top notch. So you can be as loud as you'd like."

Hot color swept across her cheeks right before she was dumped unceremoniously onto the bed. Eoin followed her right down, leaning over her, weight resting on his elbows. He brushed a lock of hair off her forehead. "You are truly beautiful—did you know that?"

She smiled. "And if I said so are you?"

"It might not be as much of a compliment," he said.

"Okay, how about a ruggedly handsome surfer dude?"

He settled in for a long, soft kiss before lifting his head. "Surfer dude, huh? Aren't those all in California?"

"This one isn't. And he's the only one I'm concerned with right now."

"In that case, I hope you're very, very concerned."

She nibbled his lip. "Let me show you exactly how concerned I am."

CHAPTER SEVEN

HIS FINGERS WERE sliding over Sari's body in a way that made her quivery. With every touch, kiss and look he'd given her, she'd soared just a little bit higher.

She'd meant to show Eoin how much she wanted him, and he'd beaten her to the punch. But it was time to show him she had a few little tricks up her sleeve as well.

Pushing at his shoulders, she succeeded in rolling him onto his back, where he looked up at her in puzzlement. "Everything okay?"

"Uh-uh."

But when it looked like he was going to say something else, she straddled him, watching the delicious surprise that went across his face, a surprise that changed to need when she pulled the top of her scrubs over her head, leaving her in a bra and her pants. This was where she got a little bit anxious, since she had a cesarean scar on her abdomen along with stretch marks from carrying twins. But she pushed that from her mind. If he didn't like the way she looked, he wouldn't be here with her right now.

His fingers curved around her waist, thumbs stroking her abs in a way that made her muscles ripple. Halfway between tickly and super sexy.

His palms slid slowly upward, thumbs moving higher and higher until they reached the bottom edge of her bra. She held her breath when his fingers went behind to find her clasp and undo it, easing the garment off until her breasts were free. Then he cupped them both in one sensuous move that was almost her undoing.

He sat up in a rush, wrapping his arms around her. Being tangled up together with him like this was heaven. And they hadn't even stepped out onto any of those clouds yet, hadn't even experienced what her body was yearning for.

Eoin palmed her cheeks like he'd done on the pier and kissed her. Slowly, thoroughly, until she wasn't sure who was initiating what. All she knew was that she was squeezed up against him, straining to get closer even when they were pressed tight to each other.

Two becoming one. She understood what that meant now.

But you aren't one.

The words whispered through her head, but she tossed them away. She didn't care. Just wanted to be with him in whatever way she could. She could unpack all the other stuff later.

He kissed her once more, then eased away. "Sari, I want you to stand up for me."

"Stand up? Why?"

One finger brushed over her nipple, making her shudder. "Because I'm dying here, and I need to undress you."

Eoin set her on her feet beside the bed, but when he went to reach for the waistband of her scrubs, she held his hands. "I—I need to tell you... My scar, it's..."

He paused before evidently realizing what she was worried about.

"It's okay, Sari. I have a scar too. Look." He hauled his shirt over his head and tossed it aside. Then he put her palm over a scar on his torso. "Does this change what you want to do with me?"

"No, of course not." She traced the faded white mark with her fingertips, finding it as sexy as the rest of him. "How did you get it?"

"Surgery when I was younger. It's all healed now."

He didn't say what kind of surgery, and she didn't ask. It didn't matter.

His thumb rubbed over her tummy right above her elastic waistband. "I've shown you mine. Will you let me see yours?"

That made her smile. Then she nodded, her fingers going to her pants and pushing them down her hips and beyond. Her panties weren't super high waisted, and while some of her stretch marks were visible above them, they weren't low enough to expose her incision.

Still she felt self-conscious for a few seconds before he traced one of those marks made by her pregnancy. "You are gorgeous, Sari. Every last inch of you."

He climbed out of bed and stood behind her, his chin on her shoulder as he reached around and cupped her breasts. The feel of his naked chest against her bare back was exquisite. Then one hand slid down her belly and dipped below her panties, moving lower until it found the spot that had been aching for his touch for what seemed like forever.

Her eyes fluttered shut, and she moaned, pressing into his caress, her arms curling back around his neck and holding him against her. He was right—her scar and stretch marks didn't matter, if what she felt against her backside was any indication. He wanted her as much as she wanted him.

But if he didn't stop soon...

She twisted around in his arms. "Eoin..."

"I know." He shucked the rest of his clothing, going over to a side table to pull a condom from a drawer. And when he turned back toward her.

God! He was like an Adonis, striding toward her, rolling the condom over his length as he came closer. He flipped her back onto the bed and removed the last of her clothing, bending down to kiss her scar in a shivery move that took her by surprise. Then he was on top of her, his knee parting her legs. Sari braced herself for the wall of pleasure that would come the second he filled her.

But he didn't enter in a rush like she'd expected him to do. Like she'd wanted him to do. And she squirmed in protest.

"Shh…just wait."

Instead, Eoin used his length to trace over her most sensitive area, in much the same way as his fingers had stroked her earlier. Slowly. Thoroughly. And even with the protection between them, the sensation was crazy. Perfect. Maddening.

She couldn't think beyond one-word descriptions right now, and she didn't care.

Her hips shifted to move with the rhythm he was setting up, just as he bent forward and took one of her nipples into his mouth, sending a surge of pleasure through her. Her body jolted against his. She needed him so badly.

"Please, Eoin."

That was all it took. He entered her, and it was every bit as good as she'd dreamed it might be. She was full, so gorgeously full of him that she couldn't speak. Couldn't think. Could only feel what he was doing to her.

With each thrust, her body moved beneath his, and she could feel the softness of his quilt beneath her, the slight scratchiness of his chest hair above her. And throughout it all, her heart was pounding out a rhythm she hadn't felt in far too long.

He changed his angle slightly, and she was

suddenly transported to a world where sights and sounds didn't matter anymore. She let herself get lost in the feeling of his skin sliding over hers. In the rasp of his breathing as it washed across her cheek. In the low sexy words that were meant for her alone.

If anyone had told her sex could be like this she would have laughed. She wasn't sure she had ever experienced this level of intensity before. Her whole being became a pinpoint of feeling as something happened inside of her. A slow coiling in her belly that ratcheted tighter and tighter and tighter until…

Oh, God!

Her head craned back as a cascade of raw pleasure exploded all around her, her hips bucking hard as if trying to reach even greater heights.

"Sari…!" Eoin thrust again and again before straining against her, his own face a mask of what she'd just felt, and she welcomed him in.

God, it was good. So very, very good.

Even as she slowly came down. Even as her breathing leveled out. Even as his movements slowed. She wrapped her arms around him and held him to her. Satiated and yet feeling like something was lacking. Like she needed something more. Had reached for more before snatching her emotions back in a sudden panic.

But she wasn't going to analyze anything right now, not with him slowly withdrawing, making her wince. She hadn't been quite ready for that, had wanted that connection to last just a little longer.

He kissed her forehead, coming up onto his elbows. "Are you okay?"

"Do I look okay?" She realized that wasn't quite what she'd meant when he frowned. "No—I mean, my hair is probably a mess and—"

"You're beautiful, Sari. Truly beautiful." His thumb rubbed over the point of her chin. "Do you have to be back home tonight? The girls?"

"Girls?"

Oh, yes. Her children. What on earth had made her forget them for even a second? Eoin, that's what. And she wasn't sure if that was from what she'd just physically experienced or from something a little more insidious. A trickle of something that might be a little more than she'd expected or wanted.

But she couldn't think about that right now because he was waiting for an answer. And right now, she really didn't want to worry about anyone but herself. Couldn't she do that just this once? Evie and Hannah wouldn't know anything about it. She wasn't even going to tell Peggy. This would be her one secret.

"No. I don't have to be back."

"Then stay with me?" he asked. "Just for the night. I'll take you home in the morning."

That was right. He'd driven her here. Even more of a reason to spend the night. After all, she didn't want to make him get dressed when he could be...

Could be what, Saraia? Making you feel more of what you just sampled?

"I can stay."

He leaned down to kiss her. "I was hoping you'd say that. Because I'm not quite ready to let you go. Not yet."

And she wasn't quite ready to be let go of.

So she lost herself in his kiss and tried not to think of anything outside of what was happening on this bed.

With Eoin.

* * *

"Sari?"

Even as he sat up in bed the next morning and called her name, Eoin knew there'd be no response. She was gone. But how?

But more to the point, why?

They'd had fun, but he hadn't thought either of them expected more than that, although they hadn't talked about it. They'd just made love twice more before falling asleep in each other's arms. All had seemed fine.

So why had she left without a word?

Climbing out of bed took a little longer than usual because the bedclothes were a tangled mess, but he finally succeeded in kicking them off and leaving the room. The bathroom door was open, and the rest of the lights in the place were off. So he was right. She was gone.

The drawer to the nightstand was open, and the package of condoms seemed to laugh at him. It was kind of ridiculous to use them, since he couldn't get anyone pregnant. But there were things other than sperm that could be passed from one person to another, and he never wanted anyone to feel unsafe being with him.

Moving to the kitchen to get himself a drink of water, Eoin paused when he got to the refrigerator. The heart that he'd colored with Sari's daughters was askew, as if someone had taken it off to look at it before putting it back under the magnet. Maybe he'd moved it when he'd gotten into the fridge the last time. The truth was he'd gotten so used to it being there that it had kind of become invisible. Until it wasn't.

Surely Sari wouldn't be upset by it being there. She'd seen him coloring with them and hadn't said anything.

He was overreacting. She'd probably just woken up early this morning and decided to catch a cab back to... He didn't actually know where she lived in Charleston.

Actually, he didn't know all that much about her life outside of the clinic.

But he'd learned a lot yesterday. That she loved water. Loved the beach. That her husband had died of an infection at his hospital.

That was the one big thing he knew about her.

And yet on the flip side, what had he told her about himself? Not much. She didn't know that he'd had cancer. That the scar he'd shown her last night was the result of a splenectomy he'd had during his cancer treatment. She'd actually asked him what it was, and he'd avoided telling her. Why?

Eoin shrugged to himself. He hadn't wanted to ruin the mood with unimportant information.

And yet she'd shared something really vulnerable about herself just moments before— that she'd been worried about him being turned off by her scar, by the signs that she'd had babies.

So what had held him back?

Maybe the fact that you only shared stuff like that with a person you cared about.

So he didn't care about her?

Actually, he did. He'd already admitted that to himself when Evie had been hurt. And maybe that was exactly why he hadn't told her anything about that physical battle he'd fought. Maybe he was afraid that with every revelation, it would bind him a little more to her.

And after what had happened with Lucy, he wasn't sure he wanted to share all those details of his life again. Even if he cared about the person. Because he hadn't wanted to get that "real" with a person ever again.

Until now? Until this morning after having the best sex of his life?

Maybe. And that scared the hell out of him.

As well it should. Because he still hadn't made the decision about biological children. And being with Sari had shown him that he didn't need sperm to be a father. She had two adorable, beautiful girls who would make any man proud to carry the title of *Dad*.

For a split second Eoin allowed himself to fantasize over what it would be like to be her husband, to raise those precious twins.

Hell! He shook himself back to reality.

Thinking like that didn't help anything. It didn't help him make a decision about whether or not to let go of having a child who came from his own cells.

And that choice needed to be made without adding the face of an actual person to the mix. Did *he* want biological children? Yes or no? Maybe it was time to figure that out.

He had a couple of days before he was due back at Grandview, so maybe he should do a little soul-searching about what he wanted in life. Did he want a family? Did he want to remain single for the rest of his life? Neither choice was right or wrong. He just needed to decide what was right for him.

So his goal for the next three days was to make one big decision. Leave kids on the table? Or take them off it forever—at least when it came to his banked sperm. In sending the facility a yearly check, he'd basically been coasting, putting off a decision that he really did need to make.

So that was what he was going to do. He was either going to write a check or give the sperm bank permission to destroy his samples. Once he did that, maybe he would have the freedom he'd never felt. The freedom to move forward with his life and his future.

Sari felt like she was moving in a vacuum. Her days went like they always did, a mixture of calm one minute, frenetic the next. Her night with Eoin felt like it had happened in a dream world.

A sexy, terrifying dream. But one she might repeat, given the chance. Except for that one thing that made an uneasy lump form in her chest.

Eoin had kept that heart he'd colored with

her girls. Why? She'd gotten up early in the morning with the idea of getting a drink and then climbing back into bed, but then she'd seen his refrigerator door. There'd been no question about what that thing on it was. It had been right there at eye level. He had to see it each and every time he opened that door.

Why keep it? Why not just toss it before he'd left Grandview that day? The sight had kind of spooked her, and she'd suddenly felt the need to get out of there. It had been a wakeup call about what she stood to gain and what she stood to lose. Or actually, what her girls stood to lose if she continued down this track.

If Sari let herself get involved with Eoin or any other man, she risked not only her heart but those of her girls.

It was as if the universe had sent her a big old reminder of what was at stake—in the form of an actual heart. So maybe she should thank him for hanging that thing up. Because it had scooted her butt out of that apartment and into an Uber, whose driver had thankfully asked no questions about what she was doing requesting his services before six in the morning.

But she hadn't wanted Eoin to wake up. Hadn't thought she could handle any kind of small talk or worse…breakfast, with that heart staring at her from across the kitchen.

So she'd skedaddled. And not only had Eoin not tried to contact her since she'd fled his place three days ago, she was going to have to face him later this morning when he came into work. She could only hope one of her patients unexpectedly went into labor and needed to be seen immediately.

But what was the likelihood of that happening? Never. It never happened when you wanted it to.

Worse, Hannah had asked about Eoin when Sari had picked them up from preschool the day after her sexy rendezvous with the obstetrician. She hadn't wanted him to make an impression on them, but evidently it was too late for that. So all she could hope was that the curiosity would burn itself out by extinction. If they rarely saw him, they wouldn't think he was anything special, right?

Had her own curiosity about him burned itself out? She'd once wondered if it would if she ever got the chance to experience him. Well, now she had her answer.

Not only had it *not* burned itself out, she wanted to know more. She wanted to know exactly what that scar on his torso was from, even though she knew it was none of her business. If he'd wanted her to know he would have said so. But she felt a little unevenly matched since he knew exactly what her scar was from.

And he'd been so exquisitely tender about the whole thing, even making her smile with his "I showed you mine, now show me yours" challenge. He'd known exactly what to say to put her at ease. And she loved that about him.

No. *Love* wasn't the right word. She *liked* that about him. There. That was better.

Just then, the door opened and in strolled Eoin, looking damnably good in jeans and a navy T-shirt. He was dressed a little more casually than he usually was, but none of them dressed up for this job. And he actually looked like all was right with the world, which made Sari feel kind of miserable.

Heidi took one look at her face and made an excuse to leave. Was it that obvious that something about the man was bothering her?

He came over to her and smiled. "You disappeared."

She knew exactly what he was talking about. And she didn't really want to discuss it out here in the foyer. "Can we go into your office for a minute?"

He shot her a look. "Sure."

Eoin led the way to the minute space, and they both squeezed inside. Maybe this was a mistake because the way he filled this room was reminiscent of the way he filled...

Uh-oh. Stop, she told herself. *Right now.*

He didn't wait for her to say anything—he spoke up instead. "I would have taken you home, you know."

"I didn't want to put you out." Liar. Was this really how she wanted this conversation to go? "No, scratch that. I felt funny about what had happened and decided to sneak out while you were sleeping."

"I kind of realized that when you weren't there the next morning." He paused. "You felt funny how?"

"I don't know. I dated someone a while back and let him get involved in my girls' lives, and then we broke up. They were devastated. I swore I would never go down that road again with anyone. And I was afraid if I stayed…"

"You were afraid if you stayed that I might ask that of you," he said.

"Simply put, yes."

He came around his desk until he stood in front of her. "I would never put you in that kind of position, Sari. You control who your daughters interact with, and you absolutely have that right. I promise I won't try to worm my way into their lives behind your back."

"It's not just behind my back," she said. "I…well, I don't want to make another mistake."

"Neither do I," he said. "I was in a bad relationship a while back as well. And I'm not in a hurry to jump back into one either. Why don't we agree that what we did was fun? And if we want to do it again, it's okay."

She nodded. "I can live with that."

"And while we're being honest…" He rubbed his hand over an area on his midriff. "That scar I showed you is from a splenectomy."

"A splenectomy? Were you in a car accident?" Most splenectomies she'd heard about had been the result of some kind of injury to the organ that could cause it to swell with blood until it burst, a life-threatening event.

"No. I wasn't in an accident. I had Hodgkin's lymphoma almost twenty years ago. They had to take my spleen because of it."

Shock went through her. "Eoin, I'm sorry. I had no idea."

"I know. And I'm not sure why I didn't tell you that night. Maybe because talking about your cancer isn't the sexiest thing in the world."

That made her laugh. "And talking about stretch marks is?"

"Yes." He touched her hand. "Because yours are very, very sexy."

Sari bit her lip. "Okay, maybe we should change directions. So we agree that everything is okay and nothing is weird?"

"'Nothing is weird' as in nothing is off limits?"

She swatted his arm. "You know what I meant." But she loved that he could joke about it. It made running off like she had seem a little bit ridiculous. He was showing her there was nothing to be afraid of.

"I did. But your face turns pink right here

in a way that fascinates me." His fingers slid over her cheek.

Wow. She fascinated him?

Well, he certainly fascinated her as well.

"And your cancer is cured?" The words came out before she could stop them. And she wasn't sure why they even came to mind.

"That's what they tell me," Eoin said. "There's been no sign of it recurring anyway, although a splenectomy means I might get some other type of lymphoma at a later date."

He was so matter-of-fact about it, as if it weren't important. And maybe if you'd been facing something like this your whole life, it became almost normal.

But it wasn't. And "some other type of lymphoma" probably meant one that was more aggressive, although he hadn't specified that. It wasn't her area of expertise and she didn't feel right grilling him with questions about his health, so she decided to leave it be.

After all, like he'd said, they were just having fun. There was no commitment. No need to wonder about what their future together might hold. Or might not.

In a way it was freeing. Because with Max, she'd been constantly analyzing everything he'd said as things started heading south between them.

She didn't need to do that here. And Eoin had promised to keep Evie and Hannah out of it if that was what she wanted. It was. She thought so anyway.

"Well, I'm glad you beat it. Because I can't imagine the world without you, Eoin Mulvey."

She hadn't been able to imagine the world without David either, but there you had it. You didn't always get your wish.

"Thanks," he said. "I'm kind of glad to still be here in it. Even if beautiful women run out on me in the middle of the night."

She laughed. "It was morning, mister!"

"Same difference." His face turned serious. "I woke up, and you were gone. I didn't much like that feeling, so please don't do it again."

Said as if they might spend the night together again. She liked that, although her daughters didn't spend the night with Peggy more than about once a month. And it would be hard to ask her to without offering up some kind of explanation. But Sari also didn't want to say no to him. So she took some middle ground.

"If I'm ever at your place again, I promise not to leave next time without at least waking you up before I go-go."

Eoin groaned as he realized she'd recited some song lyrics. Then he took her hands in his. "I hope there is a next time."

"I hope so too." She squeezed his hands and then let go. "So we're good?"

"We're good. Now, we should probably get out of here before Heidi or one of your other midwives get the wrong idea about us." He raised a brow. "Except it wouldn't exactly be wrong, would it?"

"No, which means we definitely should leave while we each still have some plausible deniability," she said.

Eoin pulled her in for a quick peck on the cheek. "I have to tell you—I'd be hard pressed to deny anything that happened the other night."

But he reached around her and pulled the door open. "So what's on the docket today?"

As they left his office, the conversation turned back to what the clinic's schedule looked like today. And Sari was glad. So very glad that they'd gotten things settled between them.

Even if they were no closer to putting a definition to what they'd done than they had four days ago. Other than "fun."

Their night together had been fun. And maybe there was no need to define it past that. At least not for today.

CHAPTER EIGHT

EOIN HAD SURVIVED his first water birth.

Well, *he* hadn't, but Sari's patients had. Both of them. They'd offered to let him observe, and Sari had taken him aside and asked him to make sure that he didn't put on his doctor hat unless she specifically asked him to.

He had to admit it was a nerve-racking experience, even as an observer. He'd held his breath the whole time the baby had been born beneath the water's surface, even though he'd mentally known that the cord had been providing all the oxygen that the baby had needed. And the infant had been out of the water and onto his mom's chest pretty quickly.

Water births weren't new by any means. His own hospital was even thinking of putting in a birthing tub in the maternity ward. But Eoin would never get to use one. Not because he disagreed with them, but because by the time the patients reached his office, any kind of natural birth was off the table. Survival was the name of the game.

The method was certainly not without its critics. And many of those detractors were in his own field.

It was obvious that Sari really believed in this. She'd coached the mom through the whole process, all the way down to letting the mom and dad catch their own baby.

Watching her in that role was amazing. Her passion. Her belief. The way she tirelessly advocated for her patient. It made something in Eoin tighten with some unknown emotion. But he felt damned proud that he'd been here to witness this.

Everyone seemed healthy and happy with the process. Sari measured and weighed the baby once the mom was ready. Skin-on-skin time was very important at the clinic, and she let them set their own time frame as far as how long that lasted. If it had taken hours, Eoin had no doubt that she would have been fine with that.

Once everyone was out of the tub, the mom glanced his way, and he stepped forward and congratulated them, thanking them for letting him be in the room during this special occasion.

"Was it what you expected?" she asked.

"No, but it was a beautiful process, and I'm glad Grandview offers the option."

"We are too." She smiled. "We're so happy a friend recommended we check it out. And Saraia has been wonderful throughout the whole pregnancy. We'll probably have our next child here as well."

Next child. As if that were just a given. He'd thought all week about what to do with his banked sperm, and after his thoughts about Sari and being a dad, he realized he wasn't as opposed to it as he'd been back when he and Lucy had been together. In fact it had looked damned attractive the morning after he and Sari had made love. And he realized with the right person, he might just want to don that *Dad* title. So he'd decided to pay for another year. Not just to put off deciding like he'd done in the past, but to really use this as a springboard for what the future could hold.

Might that have been partly because of his night with Sari?

Yes, he thought so. Thought it might actually happen someday. But what he wasn't saying was that he was pinning any of his hopes on Sari. Because he wasn't. Even this morning, she'd been honest, saying she wasn't sure she wanted someone in her girls' lives—now or maybe ever. And he could respect that.

Once he and Sari left the room to let the new little family get acquainted, she said, "So, what did you really think?"

"I'm thinking it was pretty far out of my comfort zone. But certainly not out of theirs. Or yours."

"I don't do a ton of these, but no matter how a baby is born, it's always a pretty miraculous event," she said. "Mine wasn't ideal, but I'm still glad for the experience. Still glad for two healthy girls."

"Do you think you'll ever have more children?" he asked.

She paused, as if not sure how to answer. "I don't know, honestly. Next year, when I turn thirty-five, I'll be considered a higher-risk patient in most obstetricians' books."

"How about in most midwives' books?"

"It's not out of the realm of possibility to still give birth at Grandview, but there would be tests to check for birth defects. And after a C-section it's riskier to have a natural birth. It depends on the state of my uterus, especially after twins. It's not something I let myself think a lot about." She shrugged. "Maybe it's another reason I went into midwifery. To help other women get what I didn't."

"I can definitely understand that," Eoin said.

She smiled and touched his hand. "I'm glad. Now, I need to go and get some paperwork done on this birth. See you later?"

"I'll be around."

With that, Sari sauntered down the hallway, looking like she didn't have a care in the world. But he did. Because despite the little pep talk he'd given himself about kids and not letting himself get caught up in casting Sari into any kind of role in that, he suddenly realized he might have already done so. And if that were the case, he was in big trouble.

He might have said not even five hours ago that they were just having fun, but after watching her partner with that couple, he realized it was no longer true. Because during that water birth, something else had been born as he'd watched Sari work, as he'd watched her absolutely take care of her patients with a compassion that made them want to come back and experience it all over again.

Just like him. He wanted to experience her again. Not just the sex. But the whole package.

And exactly what was that?

He wasn't sure. But maybe he'd just gotten his answer about whether or not he wanted to be a father. He did. And it didn't involve sperm stored in some kind of ice vault.

The way his heart had been for the last twenty years? Lucy hadn't been able to chisel her way to it, but he was pretty sure Sari—in the short time he'd known her—had done exactly that without even trying. Without even wanting to.

Hell. *He* hadn't wanted her to either, but… it was done. And what was done couldn't be undone, no matter how much he might wish otherwise.

He loved her. He'd done something he'd promised himself he wouldn't do: fall for someone without giving it just as much consideration as he'd given his banked sperm.

Only this was more important than whether or not he chose to have children in the future.

This was about his future itself. His and Saraia's.

She'd made it pretty clear how she felt about men coming into her girls' lives. It would take a certainty that he wasn't going to just disappear like her ex. Or her late husband. And Eoin wasn't sure he was the one who'd be able to give that to her. After all he'd had cancer once. He was at a higher risk for a recurrence. She might not even want to take a chance on being with him.

Time would tell. But one thing he wasn't going to do was put his feelings into the driver's seat and let himself pressure Sari into giving more than she wanted to give. This was her life, her choice. And in the end, all he could do was let her decide how far she allowed him in her life, how close she allowed him to get to Evie and Hannah. And that would take time and trust. Two things he wasn't quite sure he'd earned yet.

Sari took her time filling out her paperwork. Eoin had taken that water birth a whole lot better than she'd expected him to. What she hadn't expected, though, was for him to ask her about whether or not she wanted children in the future. Was it just an idle curiosity?

Sitting at her open cubicle, she pulled up information on Hodgkin's lymphoma. She was surprised at how very little she actually knew about it. For example, she was surprised that they'd taken his spleen.

Resting her chin in her palm, she started to read through the information, but just then she spotted Eoin walking down the hallway and quickly shut down the screen. For some reason she'd thought he'd be in his office. But why? He didn't really have anything he needed to do there, unless they called him into service.

He spotted her and came over, and her chin dropped off her hand. Sari felt guilty, as if she'd just done a Google search on the man himself, looking for dirt. She hadn't been, but it might be crossing a line of prying into his personal life, even though she hadn't been going through his specific medical records.

She forced a smile when his glance went to the computer screen. "Hey, what's up?"

"I need to go back to Portland Lakes."

Her heart jolted. "Permanently?" She wasn't sure why she'd said that. She just knew that she was rapidly getting used to his presence at the clinic. A little too used to it.

"No." This time Eoin frowned as he looked at her a little bit more closely. "I have a patient with twins who thinks she might be experiencing labor before her planned delivery date. I need to go check her."

"Is she having a cesarean?"

"Yes, it's her second set of twins and she has some fibroids that weren't removed near her cervix, making it tricky to get the babies out past them."

"I see." And she really did.

"Do you want to watch the birth if it comes down to the fact that she really is in early labor?" he asked. "We have an observation room over the surgical suite. It might give you more of an idea of what I do and why I do it."

Sari glanced at her watch. It was just past two. "Can you call me if it comes down to it? I need to pick the girls up from preschool at four. If it looks like it might be later than that, I can see if Peggy might be available to watch them. She does sometimes if I have a patient who comes in during my off hours."

"I'll leave that up to you. Just thought you might be interested," he said. "But if watching a cesarean brings back bad memories, I'll completely understand."

"No, I don't think it will. I've come to think of every live birth as a success story. I just want moms to be able to have some say in the birthing process itself. But I know in some cases that isn't feasible or even possible."

"This is one of those, I promise," Eoin said. "I don't ever take the lazy way out. If I ever did, it would mean I've been doing this too long and need to hand the reins over to someone else. But I hope that doesn't happen for a long time."

"I don't think it will." She couldn't imagine him being lazy about anything. Especially not his job. "Let me know about your patient, and make sure she's okay with someone watching. And I'll get in contact with Peggy."

"Sounds good. See you."

"See you." She reached and squeezed his hand, holding it for a bit longer than necessary. "And good luck."

As soon as he was gone Sari hesitated, her finger over the button that would restore the screen she'd been reading. She bit her lip. Was what she was doing right?

Hadn't she mulled over how she'd become

so much more sober and cautious in the last little while and how she needed to maybe throw some of that to the wind and allow a little impulsivity to peek through periodically? Hadn't Peggy hinted at that during their visit to Beverly's ice cream shop?

Maybe. But Sari wanted her impulsiveness to be tempered with reality and to weigh her decisions in light of that reality.

So she clicked open the screen and began to read. Lymphoma and other cancers were certainly on the radar after Hodgkin's lymphoma, depending on the treatment that had been used. And evidently the spleen wasn't always removed after the diagnosis was made. But according to the article, lymphoma cells could enter the spleen and cause it to swell to a dangerous point, and so a splenectomy was sometimes advised.

The word *splenectomy* was in blue font, meaning she could click on it to learn more. She almost scrolled past it, but something made her aim the cursor in its direction and push a button.

Up came a new screen that gave the information on splenectomy.

There was a bunch of technical stuff about

how and why the organ was removed and the risks of the surgery itself. Nothing helpful here. Sari started to go back to the previous page, when something caught her eye.

There was a section on precautions to take after having a splenectomy. At first she thought it was more postoperative information, but no, it wasn't. It was information on how to prevent infections. There was a whole laundry list of items ranging from wearing gardening gloves while working in the yard to getting a flu shot and carrying a card that identified you as being asplenic…or not having a spleen. Because without a spleen you were at risk of getting a serious infection. The type of infection that could rapidly progress to…*sepsis.*

Sari blanked out the screen before any more words could penetrate her brain. God! Even seeing that word in print brought back memories that were too painful to bear. Of David lying in that hospital bed. Of the hopelessness of his condition.

She closed her eyes and wished she had never looked, had never even typed *lymphoma* into her search engine.

But Eoin wasn't David, and he'd lived for

twenty years without having a serious infection. At least he'd never mentioned one. But who knew if he had or hadn't.

She pulled in a deep breath. Okay, she needed to stop before her mind sent her to dark places she didn't want to visit. Eoin was fine. He was healthy. She was going to leave it at that. And since she wasn't going to let her involvement with him go more than skin deep, she was going to paint a fantasy that ended with him having a good long life. And them having a night or two of passion that would stay with her for the rest of her life. If Eoin wasn't worried, then she wasn't going to let herself be either.

No more Google searches for you, Sari. You're cut off. Starting now.

"Are you sure you want to do this?"

For a second she tensed, thinking he was talking about their personal life. Especially since she'd just googled his cancer—something that made her feel inexplicably guilty. So much so that she had a hard time meeting his eyes.

"You mean watch the surgery?"

"What else would I be talking about?" Eoin

tilted his head and looked at her for a moment. "What's wrong, Sari?"

"Nothing. I'm just a little distracted," she said. "But yes, I do want to watch the surgery."

Despite what she'd found out, she still wanted to learn about what Eoin did on this side of the birthing spectrum. Looking back at the day she'd first met him, she realized how dismissive she'd been about him…about obstetricians in general. And she could see how wrong she'd been. He cared about his patients just as much as she did. She'd seen it in the way he'd grieved over losing one of his patients not all that long ago. And yet he had to keep pushing forward.

The same way she did. Each and every day.

"Okay, I need to go scrub in for surgery, and then I'll meet you afterward in the lobby, okay?" he said.

She nodded before impulsively going up on tiptoe and kissing him on the cheek. "Good luck."

Eoin gave her a smile that made her swallow. It was filled with something she couldn't quite identify. Anticipation of the surgery maybe? That had to be it.

"Thanks, Sari. I'll see you when it's done. Pray for a successful delivery."

"I will." It wasn't just a line. She would be praying. For him. For the mom. And for those tiny babies who were waiting to come into this world.

As he turned to leave, she stood there staring after him for a moment or two before finally moving toward the door that would lead her to the observation room a short distance away.

Sari's emotions were all over the place an hour later as she met Eoin in the lobby. But more than anything, there was a happiness that bordered on euphoria. She refrained from rushing over to hug him, but just barely. Instead, she clasped her hands in front of her and took a deep breath before letting it out. Then words started rushing out as well.

"God, Eoin, that was amazing. I'm so, *so* glad things went well for that couple. I can't tell you how many times my heart leapt into my throat during that."

Her searching the internet seemed insignificant compared to what she'd just seen in real life. And it made her reaction to the splenectomy information feel kind of ridiculous. She'd looked closely, and there'd been no sign of worry in Eoin's demeanor or actions. So she'd breathed a sigh of relief and given herself over to what had happened in that surgical suite.

Both mom and babies had come through the surgery without any issue. Eoin had asked if it would bring back bad memories of her own cesarean, but it hadn't. It wasn't as if her surgery had been horrifying—she'd just felt a loss of control that had bothered her.

But Eoin had been so kind with his patient, and Sari could tell he'd listened to her at length because they'd exchanged a few words before she'd been put under anesthesia and her hand had reached to grip his. The same way that Sari had reached for his hand in the courtyard that day. Wow, that seemed like so long ago, but really it wasn't.

Even so, she felt the same kind of trust that his patient had seemed to feel. And it made her smile.

"Things went well," Eoin said. "These are the cases that make things worthwhile."

And just like the patient had done less than an hour ago, Sari gripped his hand. "I can see that. Thanks for helping me push aside some of my preconceived notions. All obstetricians are not ogres."

She was joking. She knew plenty of doctors who were wonderful. Her work was just a different facet of the same goal: a safe delivery.

"So *I'm* not an ogre? Or I am? I'm not quite getting where I stand in this particular assessment."

She pivoted to face him, hand still clasping his. "You're definitely in the not ogre category. You're too good-looking to be an ogre."

"So you're saying I'm not hideous."

"Not hideous," she agreed.

His finger came out to stroke her cheek. "Well, that's a relief."

"Is it? And why is that?"

"Because you wouldn't want to be seen out and about with someone who barely misses the ogre mark."

That made her laugh. "I don't know. It depends what you mean by 'out and about.' Because I was thinking more about staying in."

Had she really just said that? It had to be the rush of adrenaline and relief over things going so well—because it was making her thoughts head in all kinds of dangerous directions.

"Staying in?"

"Mm…the girls are at Peggy's for the night." Wow. She was actually propositioning the man.

But something in her was humming, and Dr. Google suddenly seemed a long way away. What did he know anyway?

"They are?" Eoin said. "What did you have in mind?"

Not that he didn't already know by now. But she loved listening to him talk, and drawing this out a little longer was making her want to yank him into the nearest exam room and…

"What do you think I have in mind?"

"I'm not sure, but I know what I have in mind." He leaned down to whisper. "I want to tangle my hands in your hair and feel your tongue slide over my skin."

He didn't specify where, but her imagination was inventing all kinds of places she could lick. And they were all fascinating. But he hadn't stopped there. He continued to murmur things that made her face heat and her body ignite.

When he pulled back to glance at her, he laughed. "I think I'd better stop before someone notices."

He nudged her thigh, and her eyes went wide, catching his. Eoin nodded. "It's definitely not a mouse."

She licked her lips. "It's definitely not the size of one either."

His arm came around her, and he grabbed her to him, making her thankful that they were in a dark corner where no patient's families were in sight.

"Lord, Sari. What you do to me."

"I haven't even started yet," she said. "So the sooner we get out of here…"

They used his car again to head back to his house, and memories of their last time there were swirling around her. None of them had faded. They were all just as stunning and brilliant as the real thing had been.

Because it had been real. And she'd been with him. And it was so far beyond any fantasy that she might have had about him that she had nothing to compare it to.

She let her hand rest on his thigh as he drove, her thumb stroking over the corded muscles beneath the fabric of his slacks. How could so much gorgeousness be housed in one human form?

His hand came down on hers. "Careful. I want to get there in one piece."

The fact that a simple caress could turn him on was heady. Too heady. And she was suddenly desperate to get to the apartment.

Fortunately, five minutes later, they'd rolled into his parking lot and left the car behind. In the elevator, Eoin put his arms around her and pulled her back against him, leaning down to nuzzle the side of her neck. Her eyes closed as sensations washed over her, just like last time. He knew just how to touch her to make her come alive.

Then they were in his apartment, and Sari's eyes automatically went to his refrigerator to see if that red heart was still there on display. It was. But this time its presence didn't shock her like it had the last time. Maybe because she'd already geared herself up to seeing it again.

"Do you want something to drink?"

"A glass of wine, if you have it?" She wasn't sure why, but she wanted to slow this down just a little now that she was here. Their last time together had been so frantic and all-consuming that she wanted her brain to be a little more engaged this time. By asking for wine? That made no sense whatsoever. But it was all she could think of.

Eoin went over to a bar area in the corner and went behind it. "Red or white?"

"Red."

He poured her a wine, then poured himself some amber-colored liquid from a decanter. He motioned her to the couch. She chose a spot and hoped to hell that he sat next to her, which he did.

They sipped together in silence for a moment or two before he glanced at her. "Sari... are you sure you want to be here? I can always take you back to the hospital."

Did he think she'd changed her mind? "No, I just..." How could she put into words what she hadn't even realized until she stepped into his home again? "I don't want it to go by too fast."

His body seemed to relax into the sofa. "That I can understand. I don't want it to go by too fast either. We can take things nice and slow." Eoin smiled. "After all, we have all night. You set the pace."

Maybe if she didn't let herself lose total

control, she wouldn't feel so panicked when it was over. Was that from the fear of him disappearing from her life? She wasn't sure. What she did realize was that something more than that picture had spooked her last time. Maybe her fear of caring too much.

Too late. She was pretty sure she already cared far too much. But he was letting her set the pace. Maybe not just for tonight, but for where things led after tonight. She still wasn't sure about that part, but what she did know was that she wanted to be here, wanted him to make love to her. And she would accept the consequences for that decision.

Hopefully, like Eoin's surgery tonight, whatever happened would have a successful outcome. One that she wouldn't look back on and regret.

Taking one last sip of her wine, she set it down on the coffee table and turned toward him. "So it's okay to go slow?"

"It's okay." He set his own drink down and linked his fingers with hers. "Because slow or fast, we've already proven it can be good. So very good."

With that, he kissed her, slow and easy, and suddenly she knew he was right, knew that tonight was going to overwhelm her the way it had the last time they'd been together. But like that picture on the refrigerator, this time she was prepared for that possibility. And she was ready to face it, come what may.

Eoin rolled off Sari, his breath rasping in his lungs, but tugged her so that she wound up on top of him. He couldn't stand not being in close contact with her. Couldn't stand not touching her, even after what they'd just done. He reached up to kiss her earlobe, still trying to suck down enough air to speak. "That… was…phenomenal."

She laughed. "Do you always do this after a successful delivery?" She trailed her fingertips across his cheeks and down the sides of his face, using short soft strokes. The light pressure felt wonderful. And hell, if she didn't sound a whole lot more composed than he felt.

"Mm…feels good." She'd asked him something. Oh, yeah, about what he did after surgery. "No. Almost never. I'm too wiped out, normally."

She kept up her ministrations, leaning over,

her breasts coming tantalizingly close to his mouth. "But not this time?"

"No. You energize me." It was true. He'd been on a high from those two babies emerging from their mother, squalling and kicking and pink. There'd been a few tense moments when the uterus had started to show signs of failure and they'd needed to get in there quickly and take the babies. It all had turned out well. But the parents had determined this would be their last pregnancy, and he affirmed them in that decision. The mother's fibroids would continue to give her problems, and the next time they might not be so lucky.

"I do, do I?" Sari asked.

"Yes, you do." He tunneled his fingers into her hair and gently massaged her scalp. Eoin was having a hard time finding words that weren't trite or over the top. But he'd come to a decision over the course of the day—he wanted Sari in his life.

The thing was he wasn't sure she wanted the same thing. And he had no idea how to even go about asking. If she didn't want more children, that was fine. He wasn't married to that concept. What he was becoming married to was the idea of sharing his life with her and Evie and Hannah. If he could get past her fears and convince her that he wanted all of them. Not just her.

He wasn't sure why her ex had made the decision to walk away, but he was damned sure he wouldn't do the same thing, unless she gave him no other choice. It might've been early, but Eoin was ready and willing to stand and fight for her affection. He just needed to know that there was at least a chance for them, that she would at least consider the idea.

She leaned into his touch. "You're good at more than just surgery."

"Am I?" He moved his hand to her back, using a gentle touch to stroke down her spine, all the way to the top of her buttocks.

"You know you are. But if you're not careful…"

He reached down to cup her behind and settle her more firmly against him. "Do you want me to be careful?"

Sari buried her face against his shoulder. "I think I want you however I can get you."

He went still, wondering if she was saying more than she realized. "Do you mean that?"

Up came her head, and she met his eyes.

The tiniest flash of wariness showed as shallow furrows between her brows. "Are we still talking about sex?"

Eoin needed to pick his words carefully, but they suddenly all seemed out of reach. He finally settled for, "We are. But I also want to talk about more than just sex."

He held his breath as he watched her face.

The smile he'd hoped for didn't appear, but something did change in her expression. He just couldn't tell what it meant.

"More. As in…"

"As in do you think you'll ever want more than this? With me."

Sari sat up in a hurry, and his hands fell away. "I thought we'd talked about this. Or at least agreed that neither of us were anxious to be back in a relationship."

Damn. He'd bungled it. He should have kept his thoughts to himself. But in reality, he wasn't sure—despite what they'd talked about—that he wanted to continue just having casual encounters with her if there was no chance of more. He loved her, and his heart was becoming more and more entangled in that emotion, to the point that he wanted to include the girls in any future outings they had. And he'd love the opportunity to teach them to love the water as much as he did. Even wanted to teach them to surf, if they were interested in that.

"We did talk about it," he said. "I just… care about you and would like to explore where that might take us. What a future together might look like."

Sari gave a visible swallow and pulled the sheet up to cover herself. A sign of protecting herself? "I can't think about this right now, Eoin. I just can't." Her eyes went to the door, and he knew she was looking to escape again.

Was this what she would do every time they were together, as soon as they finished having sex? Look like she couldn't wait to get away from him?

Not so good for Eoin's ego. But more than that, this time it was like a knife to the heart. Especially since she'd said she wouldn't do it again, wouldn't disappear into the night.

Maybe he should just cut his losses while he could. "You talked about your fear with the girls and what happened with your ex, and I get that. But is it possible to leave them out of it for the moment and just explore things between us?"

"There are things that I can't…risk, Eoin."

"Like what?" Maybe if he understood what she was so afraid of, they could work through it together. "Tell me. Maybe I can help."

"You can't. And I can't afford not to take Evie and Hannah into consideration for whatever move I make. It's not fair to them," she said. "They've already suffered so much… loss. To go through that again, well… God, I knew this was a mistake."

She got up and started getting dressed, her movements jerky and fast. The top of her scrubs was inside out, and she had to take the garment off and right it before putting it on again. "This isn't a good idea. For either of us." She shook her head, the shimmer of tears visible in her eyes.

He got out of bed and took her hand. "Slow down for a minute, Sari. Can we at least talk about this?"

"No. Just no. Talking won't change reality."

"The reality of what?"

She didn't answer, just shoved her feet into her shoes and hurried into the living room. Eoin could hear her collecting her purse and knew he should go offer her a ride. But he already knew she'd turn him down if he even tried.

It was like last time, and yet it wasn't. Because this time he was wide awake, but he wasn't going to make a move to stop her. Because if she couldn't get past whatever she was so scared of, there was no future for them. Now or ever. And the sooner he accepted that, the sooner he could move past her and do his best to forget tonight had ever happened.

CHAPTER NINE

TWO DAYS LATER, Eoin had evidently called the clinic and said he couldn't make it in that day. He didn't give an explanation or a return date, and Heidi and Miranda were throwing possible explanations for his absence back and forth.

Sari was almost certain she knew, and if she was right, he probably wouldn't come back to Grandview. Ever. She hadn't thought about what the repercussions of their last night together might hold for the clinic. She'd naively thought they could just go their separate ways and work on how to go back to being colleagues.

Except on some level, she'd thought he might try to call and coax her to think about it some more. But that wouldn't help. Because the more she thought, the more terrified she became. Not only because of Evie and Hannah, but for herself.

The implications of Eoin's splenectomy made her realize just how scary it would be to live with—or be married to—him. She'd lived through the loss of one husband. She didn't think she'd survive losing a second one. All it would take was one stray microbe, one instance of not being careful enough, of not taking precautions. It could even be something she carried to him from the clinic.

Her initial fears about Eoin had centered around Max's leaving, and in her mind, that had been a legitimate concern. But after her Google search that fear had turned monstrous, growing into a huge mountain that she wasn't sure she had the strength to climb. Because it wasn't just about him walking out on them—it had to do with him dying on them. Could she put the girls through that? They had no memory of what had happened with their dad. But if something happened to Eoin, they would very much remember it.

She finally realized two sets of eyes were staring at her.

"What?"

Heidi tilted her head. "Miranda asked

if you had any idea what is going on with Eoin. But I think we just got our answer." She stared at Sari. "It's you, isn't it?"

Could she be any more transparent? If they could see through her, then Eoin would too. And how did you tell a man that his cancer made you not want him? Especially since it wasn't true. She did want him. She was just too scared to take the risk.

Sari gave a miserable nod of her head and dropped into a seat in the waiting area. "Yes, I think so. I was stupid and let myself get swept up in a fantasy that…" That what? Could never be based on reality? But that was because she said it couldn't be.

"Oh, my God, it's even worse than I thought. You slept with him, didn't you?" Miranda's eyes went huge. "Was it that terrible? Is he so embarrassed by his performance that he's afraid to show his face around here again?"

She waved her hands at them, trying to ward off any more comments. "No, it wasn't horrible. And maybe that's part of the problem. It was fantastic. All of it. So much so that I think I care about him."

"And the jerk doesn't reciprocate? Spill the

beans, Sari." Heidi sat down next to her, followed by Miranda.

"He's not a jerk, and he does. At least he says he does. But I'm just not sure I can do this. Not after David. Not after Max."

"But Eoin isn't either of those men. How do you know it won't work out with him?" Miranda asked.

She didn't know. And that was part of the problem. What if life with him was wonderful and then tragedy struck? "All I know is that it could very well end up in heartache for me and the girls," she said.

Heidi put her arm around her. "Hey, don't we face that with each birth we assist with? No one knows exactly how they'll turn out. Whether there will be a celebration or mourning when it's all said and done. We've sent patients over to the hospital with babies who have died in utero. Nothing is guaranteed in this life."

"I know that," she said. "At least my head does. I just don't think my heart is willing to take that risk."

"I get it, Sari." Miranda leaned forward. "But if you *don't* take the risk you might never get the chance again. You might never feel this way again. With anyone."

They were right. Both of them. But her thoughts were so jumbled right now that nothing she said seemed to make sense. "I guess I just need some time to work through things."

"You've got it," she added. "Maybe. But his absence today tells me he is weighing his options, just like you are. And if you let it go too long, the opportunity may be gone forever."

And that was the problem. She just wasn't sure she could walk away from him completely. But he'd made it sound like he wasn't willing to continue on like they'd been, and she wasn't sure she could bear to walk into an uncertain future.

So she'd better decide one way or the other—and quickly.

After not coming in at all the week he'd called off, Eoin had finally opted to call the clinic and ask to switch his future volunteer days to the days Sari normally had off, simply stating that he'd had a change to his schedule at work and leaving it at that. It was true—it had changed. Because he had been the one to change it. But he couldn't go on seeing Sari each and every week after the way they'd left things the last time they'd been together. He thought switching days would be the easiest solution for everyone involved. But after trying it, he wasn't so sure.

Two weeks had passed since he'd last seen her. And in those two weeks he'd been pretty miserable. The total opposite of how he'd felt when Lucy had left.

Maybe he should get a dog or something. But he doubted even that would help fill the void he felt right now. That empty space was a vast cavernous wasteland where nothing appealed to him. Not his job. Not volunteering at Grandview. Maybe he should throw in the towel as far as going there went. But it wasn't fair to Miranda, Heidi, Kat or the others at the clinic to leave everyone in the lurch after they'd worked so hard to replace their last obstetrician.

They'd consulted with him a couple of times when a presentation hadn't looked exactly like he'd expected it to. And he liked knowing he was helping such a good cause.

If only Sari didn't come with the package. Surprisingly no one had asked him about his schedule changing the way it had. It was like they'd just accepted it with no questions asked. Nor did they pass along any little messages like Sari saying hello.

Today, Miranda had pulled him in to see one of Saraia's patients, saying the midwife had a previous commitment that she couldn't get out of.

Yeah, a commitment to avoiding him. Eoin was fairly sure of it. And yet what could he do? He was pretty much doing the same thing. He'd laid his heart on the table, only to have it tossed back at him. Maybe he should unpin that heart from his refrigerator and give it to her. Maybe there was something about that that had unnerved her. Looking back, he rarely ate at home, so opening his refrigerator was not something he did all the time, unless it was to crack open a beer.

Maybe he should ask her point-blank if she wanted him to quit, wanted him out of her life even on a superficial level. Except he'd been the one to change his hours, not her. Which told him she thought maybe they could work together. She hadn't contacted him to say so, though. And he hadn't seen her girls at the clinic again either.

Because he wasn't at Grandview at the

same time she was. The other midwives, if they knew anything about what was happening between him and Sari, were playing things close to the vest. But they would be. They were all good friends. Whatever weirdness that was between him and Sari evidently didn't affect the other personnel at the clinic. They were all the same cordial people they'd always been.

But something was going to have to give. At some point they would find themselves at the same place at the same time. Whether it was a fundraising gala or a dinner out as a team, which he'd seen happen from time to time on the calendar in the staff lounge. They would see each other. And it was up to them to set the tone for that encounter. Maybe he really should try to at least talk to her again. Not about pursuing a relationship, but to assure her that he would no longer pressure her into taking their relationship any further.

Okay, now that was a plan he could get behind. Maybe he should try to appear on a day when he knew she would be here. Or maybe he should simply send her a text asking to see her.

No, that wouldn't work. Because she'd just

view it as more of the same and would refuse to see him.

Unless he surprised her. But would that come across as stalkerish? Hell, he didn't know anymore. But one thing he did know was that he had something that he should return to her so that she would no longer worry about him pursuing her. He was going to give her his heart. Not as in the actual one, but the one he'd colored. And then he could simply ask her if she wanted him to leave the clinic. It was a pretty simple question and called for a pretty simple answer.

Now all he had to do was figure out a way that seemed as nonthreatening as possible.

Sari wasn't sure she could do this anymore. And she wasn't sure it was working. She came in each and every day and knew that Eoin wouldn't be there because he'd been there on a different day. And when she was home with her girls, she wondered what he was doing at the clinic. The thought of opening the door to something more still frightened her, but so did the idea of never setting eyes on him again.

Didn't people do cancer treatments all the

time and never have to look it in the face again? There were people who never relapsed—Hodgkin's having one of the highest cure rates of all the lymphomas. And the sepsis risk? It was there. But David had never had cancer, and he'd still contracted an infection that his body couldn't fight off. Any of them could. Evie could have died of her head injury when it came down to it. And yet Sari hadn't thrown her daughter out of her life.

She had a feeling Eoin didn't talk to many people about his cancer. He'd admitted as much, and yet he'd told her the truth, had made himself as vulnerable as she'd made herself. But whereas he'd accepted her, accepted the whole package, she'd put up a big detour sign, motioning him to steer clear of her and her daughters under any circumstances.

It had probably made him feel pretty shitty. No wonder he'd changed his schedule. She wouldn't want to see him either if he'd done something like that to her.

Kind of like Max had done. She'd vilified her ex in every way, and yet she'd walked away from Eoin in just the same manner.

It wasn't fair. And he deserved to know

what exactly she was so afraid of. And then maybe he would at least understand how he'd turned her world upside down with his presence. And she wasn't sure she wanted to— or even *could*—go back to what she'd had before.

So did she take a chance and risk it all? Maybe. Maybe that was the only way for her to know one way or another if she had the courage to face another illness or death.

Perhaps Sari would show up on one of the days he was here and march down to his office and knock on the door. Did she deserve a hearing? Probably not. But she wanted one, so she could put this behind her once and for all. So that she could decide whether her future included him or it didn't.

Just like the expectant moms Sari served at this clinic, it was her choice. She had the power to decide her future. Or at least feel out what it might look like. If Eoin was even talking to her anymore.

So that was what she was going to do. Tomorrow was his day to work, so she'd be there bright and early. And she wasn't going to say a word to Heidi, Miranda or Kat because as much as she loved them, she didn't want them inadvertently tipping Eoin off to the fact that she wanted to talk to him.

Miranda met her at the door Thursday morning, waving her arms in all kinds of weird ways. "What the hell are *you* doing here today?"

"Um… I work here," Sari said. "Do I need a reason to show up?"

"Well, no…but…it's *today*."

Something was up. She could tell just by the way the other midwife sounded. "What's going on?"

"Nothing. I'm just waiting on Heidi."

Sari frowned. "Isn't Eoin supposed to be working here today?"

"He was supposed to, but he called yesterday and said he needed to switch his day to this Friday instead."

The day she was supposed to be working. "Did he say why?"

This time, her friend avoided her eyes, so Sari stepped in front of her, forcing her to look at her. "Did. He. Say. Why?"

Miranda actually bit her lip and looked horribly guilty. "He said he wanted to talk to you. Whatever it was sounded pretty final."

Oh, God. "Is he quitting?"

"I don't really think so," Miranda said, "but I couldn't say. He could have just put his notice in with Heidi and been done with it. All I know is that it sounds like he has something pretty important to discuss with you. Just remember what we talked about. Please?"

She had something pretty important to discuss with him too. "Okay, thanks. Please don't say anything to him, though. I'll just show up like normal on Friday and see what happens."

"So you don't want me to mention your coming in today?"

She gave her friend a scowl. "No. I don't. This is something Eoin and I need to work out between ourselves."

"Well, I damn well hope it gives you both a better attitude," Miranda said, "because no one has wanted to be around either of you for the last two weeks."

Sari was immediately contrite. She walked over and gave her friend a hug. "I'm sorry. I guess I have been pretty grouchy."

"Why do you think Heidi headed for the hills when she saw you coming today?"

"Oh, hell. It looks like I owe a couple

of people an apology." She closed her eyes and then opened them again. "Starting with Eoin."

"That's the spirit." Her friend smiled. "I truly hope it works out between the two of you. I can't imagine a cuter couple."

She shrugged. "It'll be what it'll be."

On Friday, Sari entered her cubicle, only to find something on her desk. She frowned and went over to the paper. It was blank on one side, but when she turned it over there was a red heart. Her own heart leaped into her chest because she recognized it. And she had no idea what it meant. Did it mean Eoin was done, that he wasn't holding on to anything that reminded him of her? She was too late. Just like her friends had warned she might be.

She sat down and stared at the piece of paper.

"Sari..."

His voice came from the entryway to her space, as sure and deep as it had always been, as it had been those steamy nights when they'd made love. And she realized then and there that she'd fallen in love with him.

All of him.

Despite his uncertainty over some of the birthing techniques she espoused, he'd been able to keep an open mind about it.

And yet she hadn't done the same for him. She'd shut the door without even looking behind it to see the possibilities. Because she was afraid.

Sari looked up, twining her hands together as she tried to think of the right thing to say. But she came up blank.

Maybe she needed to start with the picture and go from there.

She picked it up and held it so he could see. "I don't understand. What does this mean?"

"It means I don't want to hold on to anything that makes you uncomfortable," he said.

"Uncomfortable?"

"Yes. If you don't want me in your girls' lives, I'll respect that, but I can't go on working here if that's the case," he said. "It would just be too…hard."

Oh, no. It really was too late.

"But why?" she asked.

He stared at her for a long moment. "Isn't it obvious?"

Was it supposed to be? "Maybe to you. But not to me."

He took a step closer. "Okay, I'll spell it out for you, even though it's something you probably don't want to hear," he said. "I love you. I realized it right before last time we were together, but from your reaction it was pretty obvious you don't feel the same way, so…that's that."

She fingered the picture. "Will you sit for a minute and let me explain to you why I said what I did that night?"

"Will it change anything?"

"Maybe," she said. "If I haven't left it for too long."

Something in Eoin's eyes darkened as if trying to weigh her words, but he sat down like she'd asked.

"Let me start by saying I did some reading about Hodgkin's lymphoma and realized I know very little about it. I didn't even know that a splenectomy carries some long-term risks." She bit her lip, struggling to continue. "Like an infection turning septic. The second I read those words, it set off a chain reaction inside of me. It brought back memories of David, as he died of that very thing. But worse was the fear that the same thing could happen to you at some point. That my daughters, who don't remember their dad, would have to live through something horrible happening to you."

She shrugged. "Because I love you too. And I'm so terrified of losing you…" Taking a breath, she somehow got out the rest of the sentence. "I'm so terrified of losing you that I was willing to shut you out of our lives completely."

"Was?"

She nodded. "I'm still afraid. But something finally clicked in my head. None of us are guaranteed tomorrow. I've seen pregnancies sail along without a problem, only to reach an unexpectedly tragic end. But most of the moms I've met wouldn't trade the ability to hold their infant. If I'd known ahead of time David was going to die, I'd have still married him, would still have our beautiful girls. And that is the kicker—am I willing to shut the door on what could be a beautiful thing just because of a picture I've constructed in my head out of fear?"

"What are you saying?" Eoin asked.

"I'm saying that if you'll still have me, I'll try," she said. "If you'll help me work through my moments of doubt and fear. But you have to promise never to walk out on my girls, even if we end up in the divorce courts."

He tipped her chin up and placed a gentle kiss on her mouth. "How about if I promise to never walk away from any of you? And I can tell you right now that I'm as healthy as a horse. I've shown no signs of relapse or serious illness. It's not to say that it couldn't happen. But we all take that chance when we love someone."

"So it's not too late?" Sari asked.

His brows went up. "Honestly? I thought maybe it was. I was pretty sure I was going to hand in my resignation today." He reached across the desk and took one of her hands. "But if you say otherwise, I will walk through that door with you instead of on my own."

"I don't want you to leave."

His eyes closed for a minute before reopening. "God. I never thought I'd hear you say that."

"So you'll stay?" she asked. "And let me make it up to you?"

"I'll stay. But I have one more thing to tell you. And it'll be your decision entirely," he said. "Twenty years ago, when I was undergoing treatment, the doctors asked me to think about whether I'd ever want to have kids. Like most young people, I said of course. But the treatment wiped out my ability to father children naturally."

"I don't care about any of that."

"I do. Because I banked sperm just in case, and it has sat in limbo for all this time," he said. "I went back and forth about what to do about it. Keep it stored? Or have the samples destroyed? A few weeks ago, I finally decided I might want a child someday. But no matter what, I would consider having a ready-made family made up of you, Evie, Hannah and me the biggest privilege of my life."

Sari bit her lip, a sudden train of possibility barreling toward her. "You mean you might want me to have your baby?"

"No, not my baby. *Our* baby," Eoin said. "But hell, I never thought I'd ever be with you, so it's enough that you might want me. Despite your fears."

"I do want you. And I don't know if my body will accept fertility treatments at this stage of the game or if my eggs are even young enough to produce a healthy baby. And that's the most important thing to me—that our baby has a chance at that."

"We'll talk to someone, ask their opinion," he said. "But if it does happen, I want to make something perfectly clear. Your birth process is yours to control. I will support you in whatever you want to do."

Sari's eyes watered at what he was offering her. But she couldn't take it. Not even if she wanted to. "It's ours to control. Just don't throw out the possibility of a vaginal birth unless testing shows it's not possible. I'll take your word at face value, if you feel it's too risky."

"Life is too risky, Sari. And yet..." Eoin went over and tugged her from her chair and held her close, aware on some level that Miranda and Heidi were lurking in the hallway watching them. He laughed. "I think we have an audience."

"We do. Because I showed up here a couple of days ago thinking I would catch you on the day you'd chosen to work, only to have Miranda inform me that you'd changed it to Friday. So here I am." She glanced at her friends and motioned them in no uncertain terms to clear the area because she wanted this man to kiss her senseless, and she didn't want the peanut gallery watching when that happened.

This was for them alone. To work out the details and figure out how to make it happen. After they finished making love in his apartment.

She picked up the heart and gave it back to him. "That's yours to keep. It's where this all began. And, Eoin, I never want to forget that. Even for a minute."

"Agreed," he said. "I think I may frame it and put it over our bed as a reminder that in the good times and bad times, we share the same heart."

And with that, Eoin finally did what she'd been hoping he'd do for the last several minutes. He kissed her until she couldn't breathe.

And then he did it all over again, with a promise that he would continue doing so for the rest of their lives.

EPILOGUE

SARI HAD GIVEN birth to their baby to the great joy of an ever-growing family that included her girls, Peggy and Eoin's folks, who had made several trips up from Florida. They were delighted not to have not just one grandchild but to include Hannah and Evie in that category. She was so blessed. So very, very lucky.

Their baby hadn't been born at Grandview Birthing Center, she'd been born at Portland Lakes Hospital. It wasn't just that she'd thought Eoin would feel more comfortable with the baby being born in a hospital, it was also the fact that she had still been able to use Miranda as her midwife. She'd gotten hospital privileges just for this event.

And things had gone wonderfully. Eoin had kept his "daddy hat" on the entire time, being her supporter, her lover…her friend.

And their girls had been able to be in the room with them. Although their constant questions had made her wonder if it had been the right decision.

But this would be their only baby together. It was something both Sari and her new husband had agreed on. She'd asked the minister who'd officiated at their wedding to strike out the line "in sickness and in health," not because she wouldn't stand by Eoin if anything happened, but because she didn't even want to send those words out into the universe. In the same way that they hadn't been sure she'd be able to get pregnant going through the whole hormone-treatment path, they couldn't predict how anything might go.

And it had taken a lot of work and love for her to really trust in a future together, that Eoin would truly love her girls and not see them as some sort of appendage that he had to accept in order to be with her.

But he did love them. And they were over-the-moon in love with him. Evie hadn't said her ex's name since the day she'd met Eoin that first day at the hospital. Maybe her daughter had somehow known that this man would end up being someone special in their lives.

If so, she'd been right. Sari didn't search for Hodgkin's lymphoma again. She knew enough to know the risks and knew Eoin well enough now to know that he wouldn't take his health for granted.

And *their* girls—it was still hard to think of them that way, because she always thought she'd be raising them alone—had already taken up surfing. Well, not quite. But they'd both paddled around on two small boards that Eoin had bought them as a wedding present.

It had been sweet and thoughtful and was going to be a real bonding experience between them.

And watching her husband up on his own surfboard? Absolute deliciousness. Actually, she had a hard time getting her fill of looking at him, of being with him deep into the night. Everything in her being told her she'd made the right choice. Taking a chance on them wasn't a scary experience. It was a joyful one.

Eoin carried Samantha over to the bed, where Sari was sitting up. She might've been under Portland Lakes's roof, but she was still going to do things her way. At least as much as possible.

Settling the baby into her arms to nurse and kissing her forehead, he went over to color with the girls at a small table in front of the pullout sofa. The sight made her smile.

Miranda came over. "Are you good?"

"The best."

"I have to say I never thought I'd see you give birth in a big sterile hospital room, but maybe things are changing. No one tried to interfere or bustle around the room when you wanted the lights dimmed and quiet."

Sari smiled. "I think I've made a believer out of Eoin. Oh, I know that what he does is very much needed. And every woman should be able to choose her experience as much as possible. But it worked out. And I think given my age, it made Eoin a little more comfortable having me in his territory."

"Because you're so ancient." Miranda pursed her lips in disgust.

A laugh bubbled out before she could stop it. "There were times during this pregnancy that I felt ancient. This will be our last child. I want to concentrate my energies on the family I have now—and my job."

"Did Eoin make a decision about...things?"

Sari nodded. "We asked that his remaining samples be made available to a clinic that specializes in helping families that want to have children but who have trouble affording the treatments they need in order to make that happen. There are grants and all kinds of things that I don't understand, but it's helping people."

"I think that's wonderful." Miranda smiled. "Speaking of wonderful, I need to get back to the clinic before rush hour hits."

"Go. We're fine—we're more than fine."

At that moment Eoin rose from his spot on the floor and nodded at Miranda. "Thanks for everything you did. And for not knocking me out when I asked for an update on the baby's vitals."

"You're a dad. And a doctor. It's hard to separate those two, but you did a pretty good job," she said. "Congratulations on Samantha. She's perfect, and I have to say I was right—you guys really are the cutest."

"Cutest. Okay." He made a face. But Sari knew he wasn't serious. He loved them. And she and the girls loved him.

Evie's voice came from across the room. "When can Sammy get her own surfboard?"

"Oh, heavens, honey, let's at least give her a chance to start walking before we talk about that."

"Daddy said we can all surf together."

Daddy. The decision about what to call Eoin hadn't been the easiest, but the girls knew that they had a dad who was in heaven. And between Sari and Peggy, they would make sure that David wasn't forgotten.

"Did he now?" She eyed him with mock irritation. "Has he forgotten that I don't surf?"

"He says you can still learn. That you're not too old."

That one made Sari snort, when Eoin hurried to say, "Let me just say that I never used the word 'old.' Not one single time."

"I'm kidding." She looked across the room at what she'd chosen as her focal point. It wasn't a Picasso or a beautiful island view. It was a simple heart. The one that Eoin had colored with the girls more than a year ago. He'd given it to her and said he knew it might be cheesy but that he meant it with everything he was. With everything he had. And that made it the best gift she could have ever gotten.

Because they had a love that would endure. And their family—now complete—had captured her own heart. And it would stand the test of time. No matter what.

* * * * *

If you enjoyed this story, check out these other great reads from Tina Beckett

Resisting the Brooding Heart Surgeon
The Surgeon She Could Never Forget
The Nurse's One-Night Baby
The Vet, the Pup and the Paramedic

All available now!